Remembering Anna

Remembering Anna

AMERICAN HOMESPUN

LORIN GRACE

CURRANT
CREEK PRESS

Cover photos: Deposit Photos

Cover Design © 2017 and formatting by LJP Creative
Edits by Eschler Editing

Published by Currant Creek Press
North Logan, Utah

First printing: August 2017

ISBN: 978-0-9984110-2-6

For My Mother—
For all the little things and great things
you have done to make me who I am.

Note to my readers.

FEW DAUGHTERS TRULY UNDERSTAND THEIR mothers, until becoming mothers themselves. *Remembering Anna* is the story of Lucy discovering who her mother was. A rare gift for any daughter.

During the writing of *Waking Lucy* I wanted to explore her mother, Anna, especially her love story with James. So I left Lucy with some questions about her mother and a gift in the form of a locked box.

The question has been asked "Will reading *Remembering Anna* if I haven't read *Waking Lucy* confuse me or ruin the series?"

Remembering Anna takes place in Lucy's world a year after *Waking Lucy* ends, but explains Anna's life before *Waking Lucy* begins as Anna's story is told through several entries she made in a journal. I specifically designed it as a stand alone prequel/sequel and had readers who had not read *Waking Lucy* among my test group. These readers responded that they didn't feel lost reading Anna's story first. However, I would like to point out that there are a number of spoilers as *Remembering Anna* answers questions Lucy struggled with in her life as depicted in *Waking Lucy*. That said, I believe you can enjoy the entire American Homespun series in any order that you read them.

Lorin Grace

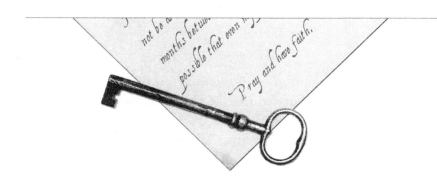

One

Fall 1798

LUCY TRIED TO STRETCH HER aching back and was rewarded with a push from her midsection.

"Now, is that any way to help? I need to finish the cleaning before you come." She rubbed the spot on her belly. She only had a few more days according to her husband's mother and only one room left to clean. Lucy waddled to the door of the room she had shared with her husband for the past ten months. Dust motes danced in the light from the west windows. Lucy was sure they just moved from room to room. When she was finished with her bedroom, they would be back in the newly completed parlor.

Starting top to bottom, Lucy stretched on her tiptoes to dust the top shelf. She dared not stand on a chair again—the one in the parlor had wobbled just a bit too much for her liking when she'd dusted there.

At the sound of footsteps echoing behind her, Lucy bit her lip. A large hand covered hers and removed the dust rag. "What did my mother say about too much work?" Samuel pulled her against his chest and gently kissed her neck before lowering his hand to her rounded belly.

"Emma told me not to work too much." Lucy leaned into his embrace, somewhat amazed that he still loved her now that she was the size of the milk cow.

Samuel turned her to face him. "Then let me dust the higher shelves and the top of the wardrobe while you sit for a moment. From the looks of things, you haven't rested once since I left for town. You know Ma will have my hide if she thinks I am not taking care of you."

Laughter bubbled up. "Emma would at that, wouldn't she?"

"You should listen to Ma. She's delivered more babies in the last twenty-five years than anyone else for ten miles." He punctuated his sentence with a kiss to her nose.

Lucy wrinkled her nose at him and stepped back. "While you are dusting that shelf, will you set Mama's box on the dressing table for me? I want to polish the top."

Samuel set the small box on Lucy's dressing table and tapped the lock. "You know, I could open this for you and install a new lock. Not even my father would be able to find the repair."

"It's not the repair. I just want to locate the key. If Mama really wanted me to open it, she would have left me the key when she died." They had discussed this several times over the last few months. Lucy was tempted to let Samuel open the box, but she wanted her mother's permission. If only she could find the key, then it wouldn't feel like she was committing larceny by opening the box. Lucy passed the rocking chair and headed for the door.

"I thought you were going to rest." Samuel pointed to the rocking chair.

"I currently have a more pressing need than rest. I promise I will sleep as soon as I take a little walk outside." She may not have rested while Samuel had gone into town, but she had walked to the privy often enough.

When she returned, Samuel escorted her to a chair and handed her Mama's box and a cloth already moist with furniture oil. "You can sit while you oil the wood. And do it slowly."

Already her husband knew her too well. It was not in her nature to sit with idle hands.

"Where is Sarah?" Lucy was embarrassed that she hadn't thought of her six-year-old sister with Samuel's return.

"She fell asleep coming back from town. I laid her down in the parlor."

Lucy nodded. It wasn't like anyone could rest once her little sister was awake.

Lucy paused to catch her breath. This would be the last day of cleaning. Then she would rest. Sarah was cleaning the dishes in the gathering room as Lucy added the finishing touches to the bedroom. Lucy knew she should not attempt to move her bed to clean under it, but every inch of her bedroom floor was now spotless, with the one annoying exception of the space beneath her bed.

Setting her back against the headpost of the bed, she planted her feet and shoved again using the wall for leverage. Inches became a span, and a span gave way to a foot as she moved the bed away from the wall.

Klink. *What was that?*

Lucy peered under the bed, which she'd managed to move only three feet. Where there had been only dirt just a few minutes ago, a faded ribbon now caught her eye. She used the broom to drag it to her, and her heart jumped when she saw the small key that dangled from the end of the ribbon. It had to be the key she had spent the last several months looking for. Finally, she would know what was in her box. Maybe she would even understand why her mother concealed so much from her.

As she reached to retrieve it, the muscles in her back and abdomen suddenly seized, and her hand closed tightly about the key, the metal digging into her flesh. A rush of warmth flowed down her leg as she straightened. Lucy groaned. So much for the newly cleaned floor.

"Sarah!" Lucy called, hoping her half sister couldn't hear the panic in her voice.

The six-year-old appeared in the doorway, washrag in hand.

Lucy opened her mouth to speak, but the next hardening of her belly stole her breath away. She gripped the bedpost, waiting for it to pass. "Go tell Samuel it's time to get his mother." Lucy tried to keep her breathing steady.

"The baby's coming?" Sarah hopped up and down. "The baby's coming!"

Lucy laid a hand on her belly and let out a little sigh. "Yes, now hurry."

Sarah dropped the rag and ran from the doorway. Lucy was sure her sister's yells of "Samuel, Samuel!" could be heard all the way to the New Hampshire border.

Once the contraction had passed, she became aware of the key biting into her hand, leaving its imprint. She needed to put it someplace safe.

Lucy mopped up the mess she'd made, finishing as Samuel rushed into the house.

"Lucy?" His voice echoed off the low ceilings.

Sarah answered before Lucy could. "She's in the bedroom."

Hat still on his head, Samuel rushed into the room. "You're sure it's time to get Ma? Should you be sitting? Or in bed? Why is the bed out here?" He caught Lucy by both arms just as another pain hit. She let him support her through it.

Lucy set her hand on her husband's chest and could feel his racing heart. "Yes, it's time. I was cleaning. Would you please move the bed back?" She didn't dare look at him, fearing he would not be happy with her ignoring the cautions she had been given.

"Did you move this bed yourself? Why didn't you ask for help?" Samuel sighed, then dropped a kiss on her forehead before pushing the bed back into place with a grunt.

Lucy sighed as well. "Please just go for Emma." The muscles were tightening again. Samuel would be worse than useless if the baby were to make its appearance before his mother arrived. He'd fainted last month when Sarah had fallen and cut herself playing with Samuel's brothers. Lucy was determined that Samuel was not going to be anywhere near the birthing.

The anticipated pain ripped through her center, stealing her breath, and she grabbed the bedpost for support. "Just…go…Now!"

Samuel's eyes widened, and he finally removed his hat, crumpling it in the process. "Do you need anything else? Tea?"

"No!" Her yell echoed through the house, and the hat slipped from Samuel's grasp.

Samuel hurried from the room, his hat on the floor where it had fallen.

Lucy covered her mouth and blinked back tears. She'd promised herself she would never yell at her husband. Like a vise, another pain squeezed her about the middle. *Hurry, Samuel!*

Lucy adjusted the blanket so that she could see the perfect, tiny face of her newborn daughter by the light of the lamp. She felt more awake than she had just moments ago as feelings of love for this new life in her arms overcame her exhaustion.

"Just a few more minutes and we can invite that son of mine to come in." Emma opened the far window and dropped the basket containing the soiled linens out. "New fathers are squeamish enough, but having one who faints at the smell of blood—well, that just makes things more difficult. I was hoping he'd have gotten over it by now." Emma tsked as she bustled about the room.

As Lucy adjusted the baby in her arms, marveling at the tiny fingers, her daughter turned toward her, mouth open and searching. "I think she wants to eat."

"They all come out hungry." Emma sat on the bed, adjusting the baby and coaching Lucy. In a few minutes, both settled into that rhythm of mother and child dating back to Eve.

Emma touched Lucy's shoulder. "I'll send Samuel in now."

Lucy studied her daughter. Would Samuel be as pleased as she was? Didn't every man want a boy first?

Samuel looked up from the board he was sanding when the barn door opened. "Ma?"

"Go to them, son."

He was halfway across the yard before he realized he didn't know if he had a son or daughter. Lucy's yelling had been replaced by a tiny cry almost half an hour ago, but he had kept his word to stay in the barn until summoned. Why couldn't he be like his father and help his wife or hold her during her pains? But the blood …

As Samuel opened the door to his bedroom, all thoughts of his failings fled.

Lucy is so beautiful. A lump grew in his throat as he approached the bed and Lucy looked up, her maple-syrup colored hair framing her face, a few strands still damp from her labor. Words gathered around the lump. The word *love* was inadequate to describe what he felt.

Lucy blinked. "Samuel?"

Hearing his name drew him to his wife's side, where he cupped her face and kissed her brow. "Lucy."

She adjusted her shift to reveal a small pink face. "Your daughter."

"Daughter?"

Lucy giggled as she held out the now-sleeping child. "Your mother and I have both confirmed she is a girl, but perhaps you learned differently at Harvard."

Shaking his head didn't loosen the lump, but it did move it enough to speak. "I'll take your word for it. Have you chosen a name?"

"I am still thinking Maryanna, after my aunt and mother."

Samuel sat next to his wife on the bed. Lucy sat forward in what he took as an invitation for him to slip in behind her. It must have been the right move as she settled back against his chest, allowing him to cradle both wife and daughter in his arms. The lump grew again as they sat there as a family for the first time. Lucy relaxed into him, her exhaustion apparent.

His daughter squirmed.

Lucy bent her head, and a loose wisp of hair no longer contained by her braid batted his nose. Samuel smoothed down the strand and placed a kiss upon her crown. "I didn't get to brush your hair tonight."

Lucy leaned back until she met his eyes, the faintest tinge of pink coloring her face, as it always did when he mentioned their nightly ritual. "I think it can wait just a few moments more, because there is someone who wants to meet you."

Samuel looked down into the blue eyes of his daughter and, for the second time in his life, fell deeply in love.

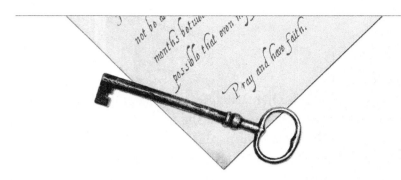

Two

MARYANNA WRINKLED HER NOSE AND yawned before falling asleep. Lucy laid the sleeping child in the cradle half of the rocker Samuel had made her. The "convenient contraption" as Emma had dubbed it, was a combination chair and cradle and was useful as long as she kept rocking. Relishing her new title, "Aunt Sarah" was eager to take a turn rocking the new little family member. Lucy beckoned Sarah over and let her have the seat.

Now, to find something to do. Emma had forbidden Lucy from housework for three weeks, claiming that the women who fared best after motherhood took a bit of a rest when the baby was born. Lucy remembered Emma insisting that her mother do the same after the birth of her brother and sisters.

There was no cleaning to do anyway. What she hadn't cleaned before the birth, Emma had cleaned after. Twice. Stew simmered in one of the pots on the stove, and the smell of fresh bread mingled with the scent of woodsmoke. Lucy had sewn enough gowns for two babies and repaired all of Samuel's shirts weeks ago. Unless she were to start a new project, there was little to do other than nap.

The key. Where was it? Lucy walked around the bedroom trying to recall what had happened after she found it. When she had yelled at Samuel, something she regretted despite his insistence that she was forgiven, the key was still in her hand. She remembered the mark it left when she'd gripped it in pain.

The key wasn't on the little table or in the drawer. She sighed. Where would she have set it? As soon as she could move after Samuel had left to fetch his mother, she'd prepared the bed. Try as she might, Lucy could not remember setting the key anywhere as Sarah had helped her lay out the things they needed for the birthing.

Her pockets. Lucy hadn't worn them since giving birth. Just another thing to untie every time she took Emma's advice to nap. By habit, she had placed them in the wardrobe drawer in those long moments between Samuel's departure and his mother's arrival.

The set of pockets was bulkier than usual—two buttons, four hairpins, three pennies, and a spool of blue thread rescued from the corner of the parlor were the sum contents of the left pocket, where she usually put her cleaning finds. The right pocket held a handkerchief, her pair of scissors—and the key.

It had to be the key to her mother's box. She looked at the bed. Samuel had changed the ticking just after her mother's death, and Lucy had changed it over the summer. They tightened the ropes every Wednesday and Saturday. Where could it have been stuck that she hadn't dislodged it before? Lucy had no desire to get down and look under the large bed, so the key's hiding place would have to remain a mystery for now. Perhaps it had been hidden in a crevice between the boards or some secret carved notch. Next time she changed the ticking she would check.

The box was heavier than when she'd oiled it last week. Or perhaps it was just that she was more tired than she thought. A little rest couldn't hurt.

After she tried the key.

Her hand trembled. It took three attempts to insert the key and turn it before she heard a faint click.

October 20, 1776

My Dearest Anna,

I will not burden either of us with how much I wish I were with you. I am comforted with your letters and my dreams.

I'm not quite sure what I was expecting in war—perhaps that we would fight the redcoats and they would be gone by now. We've had a few skirmishes, but I fear more die from illness than they do the occasional musket ball or bayonet. I am reluctant to tell you of such things, but I know you will hear tales, and I rather not mislead you. Know that I am well and safe.

I now comprehend your father's wisdom in not allowing us to marry before I left. There are many wives who follow the camp. Mostly they cook and do laundry and help with the sick. Their lot is hard, and for those with child it is even harder. There are a few other types of women among the followers, but I do not visit them. I wish I could say the same for others of my acquaintance.

The wives are forced to act as nurses both for wounds and for illness. It is disgusting, dirty work I would not want you to experience, no matter how much I long to be near you.

Lucy felt her cheeks warm and quickly skipped over the sentiments Papa Marden had meant for her mother's eyes only.

Pray for a speedy end.

Yours always, James

The next letter was difficult to read as James had written crosswise over her mother's letter. He apologized, but there was no paper to be had. Forced to squint to make out her mother's words, Lucy felt her cheeks grow warm at their boldness. She could hardly believe what she read: "longing to kiss you" and "anticipating the night I become yours." Mama never spoke like that. She had chided Papa Marden when his kisses had grown too bold. The discussion Mama had with her about marital relations when she had become engaged had been brief and almost emotionless. But in the letter, her mother spoke of missing his hands "caressing her back." Could the woman writing the letters and her straitlaced mother be the same person?

Lucy wondered at Samuel's reaction if she ever had the courage to say such things to him. If she had written them, would he have broken the engagement? Of course, they would have had to have kissed, but she had still dreamed of what their kisses would have been like.

Entranced, Lucy read letter after letter, all much the same as the first. James missed Anna and appreciated the news she shared of home, including the antics of the young boy hired to help with the farm chores and summaries of the sermons preached each Sabbath. More than one letter was overwritten in his hand, allowing Lucy to see which of her Mother's words had delighted James Marden and which had not. He took special exception to the notion that the war might continue longer than anticipated.

Tales of shortages, of arguments breaking out between the loyalist women and everyone else, and of loneliness filled her mother's letters, though Lucy was sure her mother tried to be encouraging.

The second to the last letter dated January 1, 1778, was short and only in James's hand. It opened on a more somber note.

I have been asked to go into a special service, and I fear I shall not be able to write to you as often as I'd like. It may even be months between letters. If the worst should happen to me, it's possible that even my parents might not be notified for some time.

Pray and have faith.

> *Yours Affectionately,*
> *James*

That must have been when he became a spy for General Washington. Her stepfather had told them a few stories regarding that time. Once, he'd dressed as a redcoat guard to get close to a planning meeting.

The last letter was dated almost a year later and was directed to the Wilson home. Even the handwriting was more formal.

> *February 1, 1770*

Mrs. Simms,

It is with sadness I reply to your last note. My condolences on your sister's and father's passing. This war has brought changes I fear we will all regret the choices we wish we had not made.

I wish you all the best,

> *J. Marden*

Tears gathered in Lucy's eyes as she tucked letters back under the ribbon. In the year between the last letter and this, had Mama also written about the night of her aunt's death, her marriage to Mr. Simms, and of Lucy's birth?

Lucy closed the lid of the box, her thoughts spinning. Though she'd seen her mother laugh, especially around Papa Marden, the playful teasing in her letters seemed as if it had come from another woman. Try as she might, Lucy could not imagine Mama pining over a man. Then to not know if he lived for almost a year. The same year Grandfather and her aunt also died. Poor Mama.

The room blurred. If she could only ask Mama the questions forming in her mind. She fingered the journal, but her eyes were now heavy. Already she had spent too long reading while Maryanna still slept.

Lucy dreamed that Mama sat beside her, reading the letters and crying too.

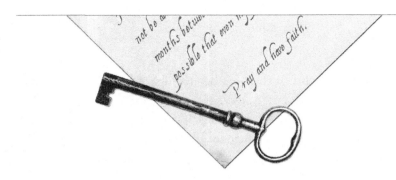

Three

SAMUEL FINISHED HIS NIGHTLY RITUAL of brushing Lucy's hair one hundred strokes. He had not missed a night since they were married, although technically it had been early morning the night Maryanna was born. "One hundred. And tomorrow I get to add one more for a year."

"A year? We haven't been married for a year."

Samuel wrapped his arms around Lucy and bent low to whisper in her ear. "I'm thinking of our *first* wedding."

Lucy batted a hand at Samuel and tried to stand from her chair. "You know very well that the first wedding doesn't cou—"

Samuel resorted to the age-old way of winning an argument with one's wife and kissed her very thoroughly.

It didn't work.

"You'll not be changing my mind that way." Before rounding the bed and climbing in, Lucy went to the corner and checked on their sleeping daughter. "Our anniversary isn't until the twenty-fourth of December," she whispered.

"According to the family Bible, it's tomorrow." Samuel dimmed the lantern and slipped into bed next to his wife.

"Only because you wrote it that way," Lucy said as she snuggled close to her husband.

Samuel pulled her close and held her tightly. His mother had cautioned him in a rather uncomfortable conversation to allow a few weeks before resuming relations. But that didn't mean he couldn't get some good kissing in. "I say I can add one brushstroke tomorrow for our anniversary."

Lucy nestled deeper into his side. "Then I suggest a compromise. You may start counting our anniversary from tomorrow, but we shall have to wait until the twenty-fourth of December until I shall mark the day."

"And how will you celebrate that day, Mrs. Wilson?" Before letting her answer, he gave her a kiss he hoped transmitted his wishes for an anniversary marker, then gently he tipped her chin with the edge of his finger and waited for her answer.

"I'm sure I will think of something." A teeny cry interrupted her. "Perhaps by then this little one will be sleeping through the night. Mama said I slept through by the time I was two weeks old. She is nearly three. She must take after you." The teasing note in Lucy's voice quickly gave way to exhaustion as she moved to pull back the quilt.

Samuel put his hand on Lucy's arm. "Let me get her. The three of us can share the bed for a while."

Lucy rolled over and tied up her shift when Samuel moved Maryanna to the cradle. In the shaft of moonlight coming through the window, she watched her husband's progression across the room. Her heart beat a staccato tempo as his silhouetted form returned to their bed. Anticipating the feel of his broad shoulders, she scooted close to meet him with a kiss before he finished pulling the blankets up. He wrapped his arms around her.

Lucy pulled back. "I love you." She met him for another kiss. "I am very happy you married me and convinced me to stay."

Samuel's answer was a long, lingering kiss. "So you agree we have been married a year?" He tickled her side.

Lucy giggled into the pillow so as to not wake her daughter. "If you wake her, you have to get her back to sleep."

Samuel kissed her forehead and smoothed a strand of hair back from her face. "I don't want to do that."

Keeping her voice low, Lucy teased. "Waking her is one of my deepest fears."

Lucy felt, more than heard, his answering chuckle. "So, what do you do in the day to keep from waking her?"

"I have been reading my mother's journal and letters."

"You found the key?" Samuel quickly sat up, causing the ropes to creak.

Lucy nodded against his chest.

"When?"

"It fell when I moved the bed, but with all the excitement, I forgot about it until a couple of days ago. I'll have to show y—" A yawn punctuated her sentence, her eyelids refusing to stay open.

"Hmmmm. I look forward to it. Good night, sweetheart." Samuel's words barely registered as she drifted to sleep.

Snow fell lightly, nothing like the blizzard a year ago when Papa Marden had died, along with Mama, Lucy's half brother, Benjamin, and the infant that hadn't been even half the size of her three-week-old Maryanna.

So many changes since then. Now she was Mrs. Samuel Wilson, the mother.

Oh! She had given Samuel a terrible time over their first wedding. It would've been so much easier if she'd just accepted it. But if giving her a second wedding showed just part of how much he loved her, she was truly the most blessed woman on the north shore.

Last night, he'd even changed Maryanna's soiled clothes again.

She would make a small spice cake in the way of something special for supper. It would not finish baking in time for the larger noon meal, but he might not expect it tonight as supper normally consisted of beans and dinner's leavings. May as well let Samuel have his celebration. He was technically correct, after all. It was their legally recorded anniversary.

Sarah set her broom aside and came to see what Lucy was making. Standing on tiptoe to see into the bowl, she exclaimed, "Dried-apple spice cake! Can I help?"

"Good guess. And yes, you can stir this while I get Maryanna. I hear her fussing."

Sarah frowned. "Babies cry a lot, don't they?"

"Maryanna is not as fussy as her aunt was at her age."

"Was I a fussy baby?"

"The fussiest. You wanted to be held all the time. Nearly wore out your brother as he was tasked with rocking you in your cradle." Lucy tapped the spoon on the edge of the bowl.

"Can I get Maryanna instead?" At Lucy's nod, Sarah disappeared to the bedroom and reappeared moments later with a squawking baby. "She has soaked herself clean through."

Lucy took the baby from her sister. "Fetch me a clean gown and cloths." Her sister scurried to comply. "Yes, little one, you are fussy and make twice as much laundry as the whole household combined, but we love you, so it matters not."

Minutes later Maryanna contently lunched while her aunt Sarah followed Lucy's instructions to finish the cake.

"Now stir it one hundred times." Lucy directed from the rocker.

Sarah made a face. "I don't like counting that high."

"Then what else can you count to?"

"Fifty. Twice. Or twenty-five four times. But fifty is easier. I might forget how many times I counted to twenty-five."

"Very good. We shall be quiet while you count."

—✠—

Lucy set the cake on the side table to cool. She could mend Samuel's shirtsleeve now, but it could wait until later. The pull to her mother's journal was greater than work. Sitting and reading would be a good rest too.

Lucy untied the love knot on the leather thong holding the book closed.

The first page was a dedication:

> To my dearest sister on her fourteenth birthday.
> A place to keep your secrets and to write the things
> you wish.
>
> Love, Mary

Lucy traced the unfamiliar writing and wondered again about the aunt she never knew.

June 17, 1775

> It is too wonderful for words, a place to write! But there are so few pages I dare not squander them on things that are only my imagination. How dear a sister to give me such a gift. I am sure she used the money from the sale of that lace to Mrs. Garrett. For all the trouble she went to, Mary should have purchased herself something fine. She is the best of all sisters, even if she moons over Welford Simms. There are so many other nice men, but some have gone to Boston to fight the redcoats. I guess she doesn't have as many choices.

Mrs. Garrett, as in Elizabeth's mother? Or Elizabeth's grand-mother? Lucy had only vague memories of an old woman dressed in black who used to sit across from them in the Garrett pew. The old lady scared her. Either one would make a fearsome client.

June 24, 1775

> *There is bad news out of Boston. There was a battle*
> *on Breeds or Bunker Hill, I am not sure which, but it*
> *was on my birthday. Emma Wilson's brother was killed,*
> *and the oldest Marden boy also. I fear that getting the*
> *redcoats to leave will not be easy. Papa says war is*
> *like that.*

How many brothers did Papa Marden have? There were at least
four she knew of, and two sisters. She had visited the youngest
sister, Aunt Jerusha, in Gloucester just last summer to help with
her lying-in. Samuel had no living uncles on his mother's side, and,
if she recalled correctly, Emma had only the one brother.

What of Grandfather Stickney? Lucy knew so little of him.
Mama's father had fought in the French and Indian wars and had
been too old to fight in the Revolution, and he had only Mama
and Aunt Mary. Lucy closed her eyes and remembered the house
as it had been when she was little, with its two rooms and its loft
over the bedroom—the same as when her grandfather had built
it some seventy years before from the trees he'd felled clearing the
land. Only half of the cabin remained now—the portion with the
river-rock oven being deemed indispensable. The old cabin currently
made up the kitchen and gathering room, with Papa Marden's and
Samuel's additions and renovations making up the rest of the house.
The recently completed parlor that was her former bedroom was
not used as often as it could be.

September 18, 1775

> *War, war, war. All the people talk about is war!*
> *Apple harvest was not fun at all. The worst is Welford*
> *bragging about how when he joins up we are sure to*
> *win. He does it just to curry favor with Mary. I hear*
> *tell he is also trying to court another on the south side*

of the river. James Marden talked to me today. I didn't know what to say since his brother died. For now, he is staying at home, but at sixteen I don't think he is old enough to fight when his family needs him on the farm. Soldiers need food, too.

December 31, 1775

So much talk of war. No one ever smiles. Don't they see the snow glistening or hear the doves call?

Mama had a bit of the poetess in her. Lucy fingered the page and looked out the window. Gray clouds dimmed the light, casting a shadow over the day. A wail pierced the air. Lucy locked the journal in the box before tending to her daughter.

four

THE DELICIOUS SCENT OF NUTMEG teased Samuel's nose as he opened the door. Sarah's smiles and giggles during chore time had given him hope that there might be a treat tonight.

Lucy sat in the rocker with Maryanna at her breast. He dropped a kiss on his wife's head and tickled Maryanna, who stopped eating to look at him.

"Oh, Samuel, look what you have done!" Lucy used a cloth to blot up the milk that dribbled from their daughter's mouth.

"Sorry, I didn't expect…" he began to offer, but as his daughter continued to gaze up at him, his heart did a little flip, and the apology was forgotten.

"Well, she was nearly done anyway. Will you take her so I can get supper on?"

Samuel took Maryanna from Lucy and made faces at her, hoping for a reaction. "Is that spice cake I smell?"

"You will have to wait and see."

Samuel angled toward the cupboard, but Lucy cut him off. "After supper." For a moment, he considered pursuing the matter. However, Maryanna's loud belch changed the direction of his thoughts. "Such a loud noise from such a tiny girl."

"That is nothing! You should have heard her this afternoon," Sarah said as she fanned her face.

"Did you give your aunt some trouble?" Samuel shifted the baby from his shoulder.

"Not me. Lucy says I am still too little to change cloths. And today I was glad." Sarah set the last spoon on the table.

Lucy followed with a bowl of stew. "No more talk of that. Time to eat."

Samuel shifted his daughter to his left arm and sat at the table. Sarah finished her stew first and looked expectantly at Lucy. When Samuel did the same, Lucy rolled her eyes.

"Let me finish, and I will get the cake." Lucy took her time with her last few bites before bringing the dried-apple spice cake to the table.

Samuel would have jumped for joy like Sarah, but Maryanna's eyelids had just fluttered shut. "Any particular reason for a cake?" He tried to keep his face neutral.

"Why, yes, there is. My husband insists that today we have been married a whole year. I say it is impossible as a year ago today I was deathly ill. But I like to humor him lest he get in one of his moods." Lucy placed a thick slice of the cake in front of him.

"Hey, I don't get in moods."

"Yes, you do. Then you go build things," Sarah said as she stuffed a bite of cake in her mouth.

A huge grin on her face, Lucy took the sleeping baby from her husband's arms and headed toward the bedroom.

"I build things almost every day."

"Then you must have many moods," Lucy added from the doorway.

Unable to win, Samuel ate his cake in silence.

⁜ ❋ ⁜

Snow fell lightly as Sarah practiced her letters on the frosted windows. Four loaves of bread sat cooling on the table. Lucy looked around the room. It was the first peaceful moment she'd had in two days. Maryanna had developed a cough Lucy feared would turn to croup, but this morning her baby's breathing was clear.

With almost an hour until noon, Lucy sat down with the journal for a few minutes of reading before Samuel came in from his woodworking for dinner.

March 10, 1776

> *James Marden asked Papa if he might see me home from church. Papa says he must wait until I am fifteen. I wish I could get time to fly. I long to talk with him.*

April 24, 1776

> *My back is ever so sore. Papa has us planting a garden four times larger than last year's. He says the army will need the extra vegetables. James stopped by on his way home from the coopers and helped for a bit. He has arranged with Papa to come help as often as he is able. Where James still has three brothers at home to help with the farm and Papa has no sons, Papa says he is glad for the offer. Welford has never offered to help.*

Lucy covered her mouth to hold in a laugh. Papa Marden was sneaky. No doubt he did help Grandfather Stickney, but he got plenty of time with Mama for it.

June 23, 1776

Finally, I am fifteen and James can see me home from church!

Is it wrong to think that James's eyes are the most beautiful thing I have ever seen? When he looks at me, my whole frame quakes. Mary would laugh at me if I told her I felt that way.

More than once Lucy had witnessed Mama blush under her stepfather's gaze. Emma had told her that her mother and Papa Marden had been in love before James went to war. If only mother had written a bit more! But Lucy understood. She'd experienced the same feelings enough when Samuel looked at her to have a good idea of what her mother felt. Could she write about one of Samuel's winks? Or about his growly pirate voice? Not that it could ever do it justice. There was no way to explain how she could feel some of his kisses all the way to her toes.

July 10, 1776

We hear more of the revolution each day. Many of the men feel it is their duty to go and fight. James says he must finish helping with his parents' harvest first. Mary is in tears because Welford wishes to go and Papa doesn't want her to wed him first. I wish she would not marry him at all. He talks to me as if I were a little child.

July 17, 1776

I caught Welford kissing Mary behind the barn. He shouted at me. It is not my fault I was looking for eggs.

He should have chosen a better place. The barn smells of animals and is not a very nice place to kiss. Poor Mary.

Mary begged me not to tell Papa about the kiss. I asked her to tell me about kissing, and she got this funny grin. Then she said she need not tell me anything. I reminded her that she asked me to keep her secret, which was very evil of me. Mary confessed that she kisses Welford almost every time they meet and that recently he has wanted more than kisses. But she dare not risk him dying at war and being left with a child, so she tells him no. I think Welford is very selfish. Mary would have to pay the fines as well as suffer the embarrassment of being without a spouse. I know that often girls are increasing when they wed, but if he were at war, she couldn't marry him.

That was one of the longest entries so far, but Mama had made up for the extra words by writing even smaller than normal. Lucy looked out the window to the barn. She had caught Mama kissing Papa Marden behind the barn, and, she thought wryly, she had kissed Samuel in the barn and hadn't noticed the smells at all. Perhaps her aunt Mary had been truly taken with Mr. Simms. There must have been some good in him, or her aunt would not have liked him.

The memories played through Lucy's mind. Even when Mr. Simms—she never could think of him as her father—had been drinking, they had food in the cellar and oil for the lamps. She knew of families where that was not the case.

Movement near the barn pulled her out of her thoughts. Samuel emerged and closed the door. It was time for dinner.

August 15, 1776

Mary has been crying buckets of tears. Welford has left to join the army with a few of his friends today. I shall not miss him. I hope she can find a nice man like my James.

August 24, 1776

James kissed me.

Lucy traced the simple words and thought of her own first kiss. Samuel had been playing the pirate with Sarah, and Lucy had joined in the game—a game that had suddenly turned serious. It wasn't the last time Samuel had teased her with his peg-leg walk and swashbuckling drawl, hoping to get a kiss or two, but it would be the one she always remembered. Had Sarah not been there, the simple kiss might have become more, but it was enough for her to know that Samuel's kisses were the only ones she ever wanted. Having witnessed Papa Marden kissing her mother years later, Lucy was sure that her mother's first kiss was something special too.

A cry from the cradle brought an end to Lucy's reading. She locked the book up again before getting her daughter. At this rate, she would never finish the journal.

Surprisingly, Maryanna slipped back into slumber after being picked up. Perhaps Lucy could read a trice bit more. She unlocked the journal and, holding Maryanna with one arm, opened the pages to where she had left off.

August 26, 1776

I had a nightmare that James kissed me and never came back. It scared me. I know he will leave in a

month with several men when harvest is over. He must
come back.

September 5, 1776

James hasn't kissed me for more than a week. I
wish he would, but we have had little time together.
Everyone talks only of war. I wish the king would leave
us alone.

The sun was now low in the west. Maryanna slept longer than
she should have, and Samuel would be in for supper soon. As soon
as Lucy stopped rocking, Maryanna stirred. Mama's journal would
wait for another afternoon.

"I'm all hot and itchy."

Lucy set the mending down and beckoned her sister over when
Sarah started rubbing her back against the wall. She quickly realized that Sarah had a fever and found a few red spots on the girl's
back and chest, though none on her face. She would get Samuel's
opinion when he came in, but she didn't think it was small pox.
Memories of having the chicken pox flooded Lucy. Better find her
mother's calamine lotion. What if Maryanna caught the pox as well?

"I think it is the chicken pox. Does your head hurt?"

Sarah nodded.

"Let's get you in bed."

Samuel confirmed Lucy's diagnosis. Neither of them spoke of
the possibility of Maryanna catching it, being only a month old.
Although chicken pox didn't kill as many people as small pox did,
it could turn deadly in some. With babies, it seemed to be either
extreme—either they died or had a case no worse than mild catarrh.

Sarah's biggest problem was boredom and the itching. Lucy tried to solve both by improving Sarah's knitting after applying a lotion of calamine Samuel had purchased along with a slate and chalk. Sarah preferred drawing to any other activity. After consulting their budget, Lucy sent Samuel to buy paper and a couple of pencils.

That same afternoon Lucy found three red dots on Maryanna's back.

Five

LUCY'S HEAD BOBBED, THEN JERKED up, then bobbed again. The dark circles under her eyes told the tale of the few hours of sleep she'd gotten the past five days. Samuel lifted his daughter and set her in her cradle, then scooped up Lucy and carried her to their bed. She had lost a little weight, but most of that could be accounted to giving birth. She was not nearly as thin as she was last year. He made quick work of removing her clothing—so much easier than the first time he'd done so, but then he had been worried about her reaction once she realized what he had done.

Lucy's eyes opened. "What?"

Samuel pressed a finger to her lips. "You need rest."

"But Maryan—"

"I can take care of things for a few hours. Her spots are all but gone, as is the fever. Just like Mama said, the earlier a child gets them, the lighter the case. Now get some sleep. I don't want to have you ill too." Samuel tried not to think of last year, but it was difficult not to with the dark circles under his wife's eyes. He covered her with two blankets. "Sleep as long as you can."

"But if—"

"If she needs to eat, I'll bring her to you. Just like I do at night."

Lucy closed her eyes. Samuel watched her for a moment before leaving the room and closing the door.

Sarah sat at the table drawing. Most of the traces of her illness had faded, but Samuel followed his mother's advice to keep her quiet a few more days. He'd learned more from his mother about being a doctor than he had during his three years at Harvard.

Samuel looked over Sarah's shoulder. The jay she was drawing was quite accurate. Perhaps he should build Lucy's little sister a writing desk. Sarah looked up, and he gave her a nod of approval. It was a fine line he walked with her—not her father, yet he had more authority and responsibility than a brother or even a sister's husband would normally have. So far there had been little to reprimand her for other than a bout of stubbornness now and again. Her relationship with his youngest brothers was a bit more complicated since she looked to his parents as grandparents and followed the boys during the summer just as Lucy had once done.

"What shall we make for supper?"

Sarah stopped drawing. "Lucy says I can't help cook until every spot is gone."

"I could fry us up some oily cakes."

"With a bit of sugar on them?" Sarah closed her eyes and licked her lips.

"I think I could do that. While I am making them, can you draw something special?"

Sarah raised her brow and waited.

"Tomorrow is Lucy's birthday, and I think one of your drawings would be a nice thing to give her."

"Oh, shall we have an apple cake, then?"

"I don't know. Lucy has been exhausted with both of you sick, and I don't know how to make one."

"Maybe your mother will bring us one, or some gingerbread." Sarah pulled out a clean piece of paper and stared out the window for a moment before bending over her paper. Samuel stifled a laugh at the way she stuck out her tongue in concentration.

Lucy closed the last of the shutters as the wind whistled through the trees. The combination of ice and snow was bound to break a few tree limbs, and she didn't want any coming through her windows. Sarah played with Maryanna on the rug. Free of the itchy pox, both girls were much happier. Maryanna cooed and kicked her little legs at Sarah's antics. The door opened, letting in a blast of cold air.

"Sorry about that," Samuel said as he hung up his hat and coat. "The rope from the barn leads to this door."

Lucy placed a kiss on his cold cheek. "I rather you came in that door, then."

Samuel caught her around the waist. "What about my other cheek? It's cold too."

Lucy obliged as Samuel leaned in for a kiss.

"Is that what it means in the Bible when it says 'the other cheek'?" Sarah asked.

Lucy pulled back and stared at her sister. Samuel released his hold on his wife and went to one knee at the edge of the rug. "Not exactly, pumpkin. The Bible is talking about being smitten on the cheek, which is a slap. Lucy was much nicer than that."

"Kissing is—" Sarah stuck her tongue out. "And you two kiss all the time. Timmy tried to kiss me again last week. I slapped him. He says he will kiss me when I am older." She shuddered.

Lucy joined them. "Just how hard did you slap him?"

Red tinged Sarah's cheeks. "Hard enough he held his cheek and yelled."

Lucy bit back a laugh. A cough from her husband indicated that he was trying to do the same. "Where was this?"

"Behind the church."

"Again?" Lucy was surprised as the same thing had happened last year.

Sarah nodded. Lucy looked to Samuel for help.

"Pumpkin, perhaps you shouldn't go off with Timmy again. But I am proud of you for defending your honor."

"Defending my honor?"

Lucy shifted. "That is when you refuse to let a man, er…boy, kiss you or do things that make you feel uncomfortable. Samuel is right. You should avoid being alone with Timmy."

"Should I have slapped his other cheek, too?"

"No!" Samuel and Lucy answered in unison.

"I am sure he understands with one slap that you don't wish to kiss him. If he does try it again, come tell me. I'll go have a chat with him." Samuel stood.

"Oh, you don't need to. Your brothers already did. That is why Timmy has a black eye."

Lucy looked at her husband and raised a brow. One of them would need to talk with Emma.

Maryanna began to fuss, so Lucy scooped her up. "Come on, little one. Let's get you fed," she said, leaving Samuel to finish the conversation.

Lucy sunk into the sofa with her mother's box on her lap. Had it been two or three weeks since she had had a chance to read? Every day she had touched the box, hoping for a moment quiet enough to read but only once had she even had time to take out the key. Christmas was still more than a week away, so maybe only two had passed. Opening the box, she looked at each lock of hair. She assumed the braided one was Mary's. The faded ribbon tied around one was definitely older—perhaps that was Grandmother Stickney's. The newest must be Papa Marden's.

Lucy hadn't thought of preserving a lock of her mother's hair. Some people did, but she had always thought the practice a bit morbid. She didn't like looking at the locks either. Dare she burn them? Not until Sarah was old enough to see the box. Lucy found one of her mother's handkerchiefs and wrapped the locks in it. Now she wouldn't have to see them again.

The journal was another matter. Lucy opened it and began to read.

September 15, 1776

> *They leave tomorrow. I can hardly write for my tears. I know it is better that we not have a king who inflicts taxes on us and treats us like cattle, but I wish we could be independent without fighting. Papa read the Declaration of Independence to us. It is most inspiring, and I know that God will be with James. But I shall miss him. I should not have teased Mary about crying for Welford. I didn't know it would hurt so.*

September 16, 1776

> *James kissed me right in front of Papa, Mary, God, and everyone. Then he whispered he would come back and I would be his bride. No one heard that. Then he kissed me again. It tasted like tears. I am determined to only cry in private.*

December 5, 1776

> *I received a letter from James twice as long as the one Mary received from Welford. But she seems happy with hers. The women are gathering old pewter we can melt down into musket balls. Father seems tired. I am knitting more socks. I hope James is warm enough.*

February 17, 1777

James writes the most wonderful letters.

Which letter had promoted that entry? Lucy pulled out the ribbon-bound letters. She should have known. It was the letter that made her blush the first time she'd read it. It had to be at least the third. Who knew Papa Marden wrote poetry? The cold nights in the camps must have gotten to him. Lucy read the next several entries, finding that most were about the letters. Interesting that Mama didn't elaborate. The few overwritten letters she had from James showed that her mother had much more to say about his letters and the effect they had on her "beating heart."

June 17, 1777

I am sixteen now. I hope the war is over soon so
I can marry James. Father is doing less than he was.
Little Billy is doing most of the chores now. His mother
is glad for the money. Mary and I tend the garden,
which is ever so big this year.

August 5, 1777

One of the roosters is missing. Papa won't even let
us go to the barn after dark. I overheard a Mrs. S at
the store today. She said there are deserters from both
sides trying to get to Canada. They are stealing food and
attacked a girl a few miles north of here in New Hamp-
shire. She would have said more, but Mrs. G realized I
was listening and shushed her.

Deserters. Anna and Aunt Mary knew of the danger. Everyone knew. Knowing what would happen only a few months later and wanting to change the entries that must surely be on the next pages, Lucy longed to scream at the journal.

September 7, 1777

Father came home from a meeting of the elders of the church. He is very agitated and insists Mary and I stay together and not go to Emma's or anyplace after dark.

November 8, 1777

I had another letter from James. I wish this war would end. All I can do is to knit socks and mittens. It must be cold there.

December 10, 1777

All the women gathered at the church today and sewed for our soldiers. Emma is with child. She smiles, but I know she misses Thomas. He went with a couple of others to deliver food to the troops. They should be back in a month.

December 25, 1777

Papa read the story of the birth of Christ tonight. He said he wanted us to remember it even if we are not celebrating Christmas like they do in England.

January 20, 1778

Emma is getting near her time. We spent most of the day helping her prepare for the birth and chasing after her boys. Junior and Samuel seem to be everywhere. She hopes that Thomas returns soon. He is late.

February 2, 1778

James wrote me such a wonderful letter. I dream of him too. Is it too brazen to tell him that? When I listen to Emma talk about Thomas while she sews a gown for her baby, I wish that could be me and James. Sadly, he says he will be doing special work, which means he will write less often. I pray each night for him.

March 8, 1778

Emma delivered a baby girl yesterday morning. Samuel keeps trying to hold her, but he is only three and is not very careful. Baby Mary is such a precious thing. I hope someday that James and I—

March 10, 1778

Papa is worried that Mary and I stay out too late helping Emma, but it has been weeks since anyone has spoken of deserters.

Lucy tasted blood. This time she had done more than worry her lip. Samuel was forever smoothing her lip with his thumb as a reminder for her to stop. Lucy used the corner of her apron to dab the blood. Her fingers hovered over the page. It wouldn't change things if she turned it or not.

March 26, 1778

Mary is dead.

Tears blurred the page. Lucy wasn't sure if she had expected her mother to write more or less about the attack that had resulted in her aunt Mary's death. Emma indicated that Mama had only ever told her the basics of that night—of the cowards who'd raped the girls and left them both for dead. Those three words were not enough for Lucy. Part of Mama must have died that night. Surely there was more.

April 2, 1778

Emma is so sad. Her little Mary died the same night my Mary did. I didn't notice. I feel so—

April 19, 1778

I need—

April 25, 1778

I try not to wake Papa with my nightmares. He looks so tired. I pray they go away.

May 3, 1778

Welford sent a letter to Mary. Papa says he will
tell him.

May 25, 1778

Emma confirmed I am with child. What will I do?
James has not written for so long I fear he is dead. His
family has not heard from him either. How can I tell
him what has become of me?

May 30, 1778

Thomas Wilson and Welford came home and are
injured. I am not sure what happened to Welford.
Thomas was attacked with the supply wagons and has
been some weeks with the army recovering. That is
what delayed his return.

June 19, 1778

Welford came by and yelled at Papa and me. He says
it is my fault Mary is dead. I can't tell him it was she
who kept us a little longer at Emma's. They ask me
questions about that night. I don't want to remember as
it makes the dreams worse. Does it matter how many
men there were? They stunk, and one spit in my face
even as he—I didn't mark my birthday. I wish I were
with Mary.

July 19, 1778

I can no longer hide my condition. Most of the
women are kind. The reverend only asked when the babe
was due and shook his head. Father assures me there
will be no charges, though the baby will still be called
a bastard. I think they all know it was the men who
killed Mary, but no one will say so. Emma tries to help.

August 10, 1778

Yesterday after church a man approached me. He
said he'd tried to stop the men from hurting me, but
that when he couldn't, he left his blanket. He offered to
marry me. I said no. He gave me a pouch filled with
money. I don't want it. I am not a harlot to be paid.
He wouldn't take it back. He told me to keep it for the
child's sake. I will use it only to save the baby. I lied to
Papa and Emma and didn't tell all he said.

He didn't try hard enough to protect me. I feel like
it is his fault I am alive. Emma claims the blanket
saved me from a cold death. Mary was lucky—no
one gives her pitying stares. Or tries to whisper
unanswerable questions.

September 1, 1778

Welford came and talked with Papa. He wants the
farm. He will marry me for it. I told Papa no. James
has not written. Please come home.

Unable to read more, Lucy set the book in the box. She felt paralyzed. Only a few entries for such a tragic year. Emma had told her what she knew of that time already. Unanswered questions flew through Lucy's head. How could a few men destroy so many lives? Had they ever regretted the atrocities they'd committed? Probably not. They were deserters, cowards, murderers. And one of them had fathered her and helped to kill her aunt. She had hated having Mr. Simms for a father, but the type of man who would do what was done to her mother was so much worse. What did that make her?

The pain of that answer was too great. Lucy pushed that thought aside to examine others. What if James hadn't gone to war? Or had written? What if Grandfather Stickney had allowed Mary and Anna to wed before the war? Her pain of missing Mama and Papa mingled with her mother's words.

Lucy wiped at her eyes and looked up to see Samuel standing before her. Odd that she hadn't heard him come in.

He knelt on one knee in front of her. "Difficult reading today?"

Lucy launched herself into her husband's arms, and new tears fell. "1778."

"Oh, sweetheart. What did she write?" Samuel lifted her into a standing position.

Lucy pulled back and dried her eyes with her apron. "It wasn't what she wrote, it was all the thoughts of what if things had been different."

"If things had been different, I wouldn't have you." Samuel pulled her close and kissed her brow.

They stood like that until Maryanna's cries forced them to separate. Samuel's words echoed in Lucy's mind.

"If things had been different, I wouldn't have you." Could something so wonderful really come out of something so heart-wrenching?

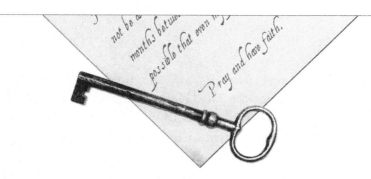

Six

Finished, Lucy inspected the garment. Was it too large? Would he like the color? At least the fabric was soft—a benefit to both of them. Heat rose in her cheeks. Best not think on that right now. Carefully she folded the nightshirt and hid it in the wardrobe. She hoped Samuel would like his gift for their anniversary in four days. He had already given her a gift, though he did not know it. One simple sentence—over and over it echoed through her mind, the irony taking her breath away. She would not have Samuel either— a man who possessed the power to heal her both body and spirit.

Samuel's father had invited the family over the following day for a Christmas feast before the twins went to attend their first Christmas dance that night.

She had plenty of baking to do for her portion of the meal. Emma had declared that with three married children and four grandchildren, an entire Great Cake was needed and she would come tomorrow to help bake it. Lucy thought it an excuse for a day of baking in her oven. After all, the two newest grandchildren would not be eating, and there had been more than enough cake last year. But then, she hadn't really been paying attention to the cake last year, and she had left early with Samuel. Making the cakes here did have other benefits. Emma's youngest four boys would not be around to steal the treats, and she didn't have to bundle Maryanna or Sarah. Her sister had counted out the forty eggs this morning and had even churned some of the butter. And now Sarah was more than ready to help with the rest of the preparation, most likely in anticipation of trying some of the sweets.

The next few days would be busy, but maybe she could spend a few moments reading.

September 7, 1778

My back hurts. Papa is ill. Welford came again. Papa says it is the only way. I don't want to marry him.

September 17, 1778

James still has not written. I fear he is dead. The wedding is set. They will read the intentions in church on Sunday. I would not do this but for Papa and Mary. I must think of the baby who kicks inside me; none shall call him bastard. That is reason enough.

No one had ever used that vile name, though a few had alluded to it, but for years she had assumed they'd spoken of Mr. Simms. Even with Emma's explanation last year of the events leading to Lucy's birth, she had never considered that Mama might have married a man in part to save her embarrassment. Perhaps it had been Mr. Simms's emphasis on the farm that caused her to focus only on the financial safety and security of such a union. Perhaps Mama had felt some of the same feelings of love for her as Lucy had felt for Maryanna when all she knew of her was her kick.

October 8, 1778

Papa is worse. Welford will not let me postpone.

October 10, 1778

I am now Mrs. Simms. I am leaving my journal and the money at Emma's since I do not trust Welford. Mr. Wilson made me a little box with a lock for a wedding present. Emma knows I am leaving my book here, but she doesn't know about the money. I do not want Welford to have it. That is terribly wrong of a wife, I know. I fear neither of us will be happy as I shall never be my sister and he shall never be J. I must never think of him again. I do not wish him to be dead, but I hope I never see him again. I could not survive the pain.

October 15, 1778

Papa is dead. We buried him on the hill next to Mama and Mary.

For years that spot on the hill had been just that—a spot on the hill. Lucy had not felt the sadness of it until Mama and Papa Marden had been added to the place. If not for Sarah and Samuel, Lucy could not have endured the pain of it. Mama had been alone. Mr. Simms would have been of little comfort.

October 30, 1778

Welford doesn't touch me as I am with child. I do not mind as the few times he's kissed me I've felt ill. I blamed the baby, but that is a lie. I think if it were

James I would not be ill. I should not think of him even if I feel he must be dead.

Lucy tried to imagine how it would be to lie night after night next to a man whose kisses made her ill. Once, when she was sick often enough to know she carried a child, Samuel had eaten an onion. But that had been different. She had still wanted him to hold her.

November 15, 1778

> *A letter from James—alive as of a month ago. Welford is furious. I explained that James didn't know we were married. Welford watched over every word as I penned my reply. When I asked if I could send the letters I had written these past months since I did not know where to address them, Welford burned them with the one James sent. I am at Emma's having a good cry. James will never know the truth of things now. And I shall never have his forgiveness.*

Lucy smiled. Benjamin, Sarah, Jane, and James Jr. were more than enough proof that Papa Marden either found nothing to forgive or had more than forgiven all. After all, what did he have to hold against Mama? Had she any other choice?

December 1, 1778

> *I shall have the baby soon. Welford keeps talking of a son. He says he has no use for a daughter. What if I don't have a boy? I hope for a girl so that I will never look at the baby's face and see one of the faces in my nightmares. Welford thinks it is nonsense to be concerned. I must try harder to not have nightmares. He has too many of his own.*

About the time Papa Marden married Mama, he sat down with Lucy and tried to explain how war changed men. Sometimes war hurt soldiers more than just leaving a bayonet scar or a missing limb. Papa said many men had nightmares, including him, and some men were never the same. Had Papa Marden been trying to account for Mr. Simms as well?

December 5, 1778

Welford came home drunk last night, again. He tried to kiss me, but the smell made me ill. It got on him, and he slapped me. He apologized this morning and said it wouldn't happen again. Emma says I will have my lying-in the next few days. She's promised to check on me daily. She doesn't want me walking here again.

January 3, 1779

Lucy is the most darling baby! I begged Emma to take her when she was born three weeks ago. Welford was so angry it wasn't a boy. He won't hold her, but he has calmed now. I consider her sweet face and wonder how she could have come from such a terrible night. She is an angel. At least Welford is keeping his promise to let her last name be Simms. I think it is because everyone knows she isn't his and it is the honorable thing to do.

The lean-to door squeaked shut. Sarah bounded into the room with Samuel on her heels. He snagged her by the shoulders. "Your boots are muddy, Sarah. Go take them off and then wipe the floor."

Sarah studied the floor and pointed. "You left a boot print too."
"Yes, I did. Because I was trying to catch you. But I will wipe
mine up. Neither of us should have had our boots on."

Lucy bit her tongue when a wail came from the bedroom. Point-
ing out that they could have been quieter was useless.

"There you go." Samuel dumped an extra handful of oats in Old
Brown's feed. The horse studied him before eating them, almost as
if he knew something was up. And something would be if the gray's
leg wasn't better. Old Brown hated being hitched to the sleigh, or
anything, for that matter. But the horse's stubbornness was not
enough to keep them from his parents' home for Christmas.

He checked on the other animals before entering the shop he
had sectioned off from the barn. The box he had made and carved
for Lucy sat in the center of the workbench. Adding the extra bit
of oil was the right decision. He ran his hand lightly over the wood
and traced the lavender flowers he'd carved there. He would give
his wife her gift tonight. The rattle and drawing board he would
save to give his girls at his parents' house tomorrow, along with the
new bowl he'd made for his mother.

Slipping into the lean-to, Samuel set the box on the shelf and
covered it with his scarf. He wanted to wait until he could be alone
with Lucy to give it to her.

The delicious scents of nutmeg and ginger lingered in the air
from the morning's baking. Sarah leaned over a paper at the table,
and Lucy sat in the rocker cradling a hungry Maryanna in one
hand and reading the journal with the other as the fire snapped
and crackled.

Lucy looked up and gave him a smile. The shadows below her
eyes were less pronounced than last week. Samuel slid behind the
rocker and kneaded her shoulders. She closed the book and leaned

into his touch. Maryanna stared up at him as if to say, "Who disturbs my meal?" then returned to more important manners.

"Where were you reading?"

When Lucy opened the book, Samuel began to read silently over her shoulder.

March 20, 1779

> It has been a year since Mary died. I think Lucy helps with my nightmares or she has them too. She always wakes me for a feeding, at least. Welford is drinking more, but he hasn't tried to kiss me when he is drunk. He wants to make the barn bigger. He says the house is big enough for now.

April 12, 1779

> I got a letter from J this week. He sent it to Emma. I am not sure he understands, but how can he with the words W forced me to write? If only we had stayed the night with Emma. But then I would not have my precious girl. I pray God can turn more terrible things to good.

Samuel pointed at the entry over his wife's shoulder. "I see Anna and I agree on the outcome of that night."

Lucy craned her neck to look up at him, and he gave her a quick kiss before they both returned to reading.

June 17, 1779

> Lucy is sitting up. She smiles and coos much of the time. Welford cannot stand it when she cries, so I

*watch her carefully. Emma is increasing again. I am
so glad that her Thomas has returned to full health. He
was so ill when he came home. I knit socks as often as
I can. I no longer send them to J, but is it terrible that I
still pray for him?*

"I think your mother was right to continue to pray for him."
Samuel bent to Lucy's ear and kept his voice low as Sarah sat at
the table drawing.

Lucy nodded her response and turned the page. "I can't imagine
what she felt to be married to a man who didn't seem to like her
and while her heart belonged to another. And if it weren't for me,
she would not have been married at all."

Samuel rubbed Lucy's back. "Sweetheart, you are not to blame.
She calls you a sweet angel. Your mother didn't find you at fault,
and neither should you."

Lucy nodded, but she did not smile. She started as if she might
bite her lip but stopped before Samuel could take his fingers to
her lips.

They both continued to read.

October 12, 1779

*I do not get an opportunity to write as much as I
wish. Welford does not like me traipsing all over the
country. I don't think he is worried about deserters as
there have been only a handful of pies, eggs, or chickens
that have gone missing in recent months. I believe he
doesn't trust me, just as I don't trust him. He is my
husband, and I try to be careful to say nothing unkind,
but Emma sees. Her new little Carrie is nearly as sweet
as Lucy. I hope they shall be fast friends.*

January 16, 1780

This winter has been one of the harshest I can remember. I don't think we have had more than three fine days put together since October. The war continues. Welford talks of going back to fight, but his leg pains him so. I hear of old school friends' brothers who have died, mostly from illness. Like everyone else, I pray for an end, but I want the king to leave us alone, too.

Lucy closed the book, set it beside her, and lifted Maryanna to her shoulder.

"Let me do that." Samuel gently took his daughter from Lucy's arms.

"Careful, she has been spitting up more than usual today." Lucy handed him a soft cloth as she stood and straightened her clothing. "Use the rocker while I get supper."

Sarah lifted her head from her drawing. "It is only beans and bread. Hardly fair with all the wonderful smells, is it?"

The chair groaned under his weight. "Oh, but it will be so much better tomorrow when we are with everyone else."

Sarah pouted. Samuel couldn't blame her. The temptation of the cakes and pies that lay on the sideboard called to him, too. He made an exaggerated frown back at her and was rewarded with a giggle.

"Do you two think you are going to cajole me into cutting one of the pies or puddings by frowning behind my back?" Lucy didn't wait for an answer. "Put your things away and set the table. If you hurry, we will have time after we are done with our beans to eat the test cake I made."

Smiling widely, Sarah excitedly rushed upstairs with her drawing pencils and papers.

"I knew you would have tested the oven with a little cake," Samuel said as he gently set Maryanna in the cradle side of the rocker, then used the cloth to clean his shirt.

Lucy rolled her eyes and cut the bread.

Samuel stood and moved to her side. "If we are very lucky, perhaps we can get both of our girls to bed soon. We have an anniversary to celebrate." As he'd expected, a blush rose to his wife's cheeks. He placed a kiss on the rosiest spot.

"Are you kissing again?" Sarah stood on the stairs, hands on her hips.

"Someday, with the right man, you won't mind it. Now hurry with the table. I want some of the cake," Samuel said, but he had other reasons he wanted to end the meal.

There would be more kissing tonight.

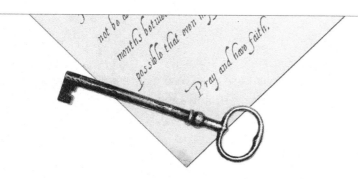

Seven

A NEW YEAR—1799. THE NEXT would mark a whole new century. Lucy bounced her daughter against her shoulder and watched the stars dim in preparation for a sunrise still an hour or more away. Dressed in his new nightshirt, Samuel came to stand behind her and lightly wrapped his arms around her middle

"I didn't get my morning kiss." His voice was still gravelly with sleep.

"It isn't morning yet."

Maryanna whimpered and sneezed. Samuel took her from Lucy's arms. "Let me have a turn. Go get some sleep."

"I don't think I can. Do you mind if I turn up the lamp and read?"

"Will you share?"

Lucy unlocked the box. "Of course."

She opened the journal and read out loud.

> June 17, 1780
>
> Is it funny that I make a point of writing on my birthday? No one but Emma marks the day. We shared a bit of the gingerbread we saved from our baking day with the children. I have told Welford that if Emma and

*I bake together, we use less wood. Since he can't stand
the cabin too warm, he allows me to go to Emma's.*

December 12, 1780

*My little girl is two years old. She is a great help to
me and feeds the chickens each day. Welford ignores her
and insists she move to the loft. I am afraid she will
fall. Emma tells me that her boys were climbing more
difficult things than ladders by that age. But Samuel
will climb anything.*

"Remember the time your father found you on top of the barn?"
Lucy had not witnessed it, but the story had been so often repeated
she could imagine the entire thing.

"I believe Junior dared me to crow with the rooster." Samuel
moved the still fussy Maryanna to his other shoulder.

"It doesn't seem that Mama wrote too often, but I know she was
at your house at least once a week."

Samuel rocked back and forth, their daughter quieted. "Perhaps
between the children, baking, and everything else they did, it was
hard to find time to write. She never did when we were around.
Junior and I would have tried to get into the box if we knew it
existed."

Lucy stifled a laugh with her hand and continued to read.

April 21, 1781

*Welford is drinking more. He is angry I am not yet
with child. I have asked Emma about it (as she has
taken on the midwifery), and she is at a loss. But she
did point out that my mother only had three children. I
often forget about my younger brother as he only lived
a few days after mother died and I was but five. Emma*

said some women just have a harder time than others.
Lucy is proof enough that I am capable.

June 17, 1781

I still do not carry Welford's child. Thomas and
Emma asked us to dinner after church. My little angel
keeps growing each day. Emma was right, thank
heaven—she has not tumbled out of the loft. Welford
calls. He must have finished his business. He must not
learn of my box.

Lucy adjusted the pillow behind her. "She managed to write
a few lines on her birthday each year, other than that year. Poor
Mama. Mr. Simms was so very upset that she didn't give him a son.
I never could understand why he would be so angry until Mama
explained the ways of husbands and the origin of babies when she
was caring Sarah. I know she could not believe that she was with
child when Benjamin was born. Did they teach you why things
happen like that at Harvard?"

Samuel shook his head and whispered, "It isn't always the mother.
Keep reading. Our little angel seems to be calmer when she hears
your voice."

October 8, 1781

Welford is one of three men taking food and supplies
down to the army. I expect he will be gone at least
three months, maybe more, depending on the weather.
They will meet up with others for protection. Since
the harvest is over, I can tend the animals without
much assistance.

December 18, 1781

My little girl looks so grown up in her new stays.
Lucy and I have been enjoying such a quiet home. I
do love how bright and cheery it looks when the sun
reflects off the snow. Even if the storm kept us inside
the past few days.

February 3, 1782

Today's sermon was on obedience. It reminds me that
Welford will be back soon.

May 5, 1782

We have finished the planting. I still do not carry
Welford's child. He says it is my fault. I know not
what to do. Emma has no other herbs I can try.

June 23, 1782

I could not get over to Emma's to write on my birthday. Welford did not come with us to church today,
saying his leg hurt. I think it has more to do with his
new horse.

August 9, 1782

Lucy's arm is broken or, rather, twisted, according
to Emma. From what I can piece together, Lucy called
Welford Papa last night when he checked on her in bed,

and he twisted her arm. During the night, Lucy walked to Emma's. Emma told Welford that Lucy must be still and should not be moved. I wish she would have taken Lucy the night she was born. At least Welford will let her stay with Emma for a few days.

"I'm glad Ma didn't."

"What?"

"Take you in. I could not have married my sister."

Lucy studied the man cradling their child in his arms, unsisterly thoughts dancing through her mind. "I am also glad that I was not raised as your sister."

September 1, 1782

I am scared to take Lucy home, but I fear for myself if I do not. Without her sleeping in the house, Welford is free to touch me as often as he wishes. It is hard to hide my disgust. At least he has stopped drinking as much after the reverend's visit two weeks ago.

"She is asleep. Come, let us sleep too."

Lucy did not need to be asked twice, even if it was not thoughts of sleep on her mind. She put the book away and turned out the lamp almost as fast as Samuel tucked Maryanna into the cradle.

Lucy looked toward the window as they settled in but quickly sat back up when she saw an orange glow there. "Samuel! Is that light coming from the barn?"

"Fire!"

Eight

SAMUEL LEAPED FROM THE BED, Lucy following. "Use the great coat, not your cape." Samuel slid on his boots, not bothering with pants or socks.

Lucy thrust her arms into the sleeves of Papa Marden's old coat. "The baby!"

"Get Sarah to stay with her."

Samuel ran from the house, confident that Lucy would follow as soon as she could. Smoke and flames poured from the hay-loft door.

The animals squealed and bellowed as Samuel opened the barn door. The goat, never content to stay penned, ran across the yard. Flames engulfed the loft above Samuel, and smoke billowed around him, but he saw no flames on the ground. Quickly he moved from stall to stall, opening the gates and shooing the animals out into the night. Though the sow wasted no time exiting the barn, the cows needed a shove.

Lucy joined him, a scarf wrapped around her face, and led one of the horses to safety, its mate following behind. Strands of burning hay fell from the loft, and flames erupted around him. Old Brown reared up on his hind legs, and Samuel struggled to bring him under control. Eyes wild, the horse danced out of the way. Heat seared Samuel's back. Lucy was beside him, a wet blanket in hand, which she tried to toss over Old Brown's head but missed. Samuel yelled for Lucy to leave, but she bent to retrieve the blanket instead, and the horse kicked out, connecting with her side and sending her flying to land just inches from the flames hungrily eating at the stall wall.

Samuel lifted Lucy in his arms and ran from the barn. He tried to whistle for his faithful horse, but only a cough came out. Setting Lucy next to the pump, he wet another blanket and ran back into the burning barn. Succeeding where Lucy had not, he got the blanket settled over Old Brown's head, then guided his horse through the flames and out into the yard.

Hearing a sudden roar, Samuel turned to see the roof of the barn collapse. Samuel released Old Brown and ran to his wife's side. The air burned in his throat, and each cough came out raspy.

Lucy clutched her side. "Oh, Samuel, why didn't you cover your face?" She reached up and touched his cheek.

Samuel found he couldn't answer. He only shook his head.

A hen ran between them. Lucy must have released them from the coup.

Gathering his wife in his arms, he moved them to the porch, where Sarah stood watching the flames. Old brown and the other two horses huddled under the trees near the lane. The cow stood in the muddy garden plot. The goat was nowhere to be seen.

An icy rain began to fall, but too late to save the barn or his shop. Inside Maryanna slept through it all.

Sunshine bounced off the two-foot-high snowdrifts outside, brightening the room. Ironic that two days of the fiercest storms had resulted in the house being better lit than in midsummer. Corners that were usually dim could be plainly seen, and all seemed to harbor dust piles or a spider web. Lucy spent the morning taking advantage of the light and scrubbed places that her broom had missed since Maryanna was born nearly three months ago. The smell of ham and beans and baking bread filled the house.

Outside, Samuel and his father, Thomas, and the younger brothers sifted through the remains of the barn, hoping to salvage at least some of the woodworking tools. Occasionally a shout would go up and someone would hold a file or rasp high, its wooden handle either charred or burned off completely. The animals, other than the chickens, whose coop remained intact, were being housed at nearby farms. A still-skittish Old Brown was taken to the stall he had been raised in at Samuel's parents' farm.

In the other room, Sarah's giggles came from the chair cradle. She had been assigned to rock the baby to sleep, but neither seemed inclined to it. Lucy ran a dustcloth over her mother's box. With the girls occupied, she figured she could spare a few moments to read.

June 17, 1783

The war is over. I heard a rumor that J is alive. I hope he will be happy. Emma has borne twin boys.

October 10, 1783

Was shopping with Emma and saw James's sister Betsy. She informed us that James is working down in Virginia. The way she looked at me, it was as if it was my fault. It isn't. I thought he was dead. Papa was dying, and I had no choice. I could not run the farm alone and with a baby. But I could not say that to her.

February 24, 1784

We have enjoyed several peaceful weeks. The new barn is complete, and Welford is quite pleased. Lucy is careful to call him Mr. Simms and stays out of his way as much as possible. I am still without child. Welford says those men ruined me.

More than he will ever know.

Lucy tried not to think of what Mr. Simms would say if he could see his beloved barn now. Undoubtedly he would find a way make the fire Lucy's fault. Thomas guessed that some of the hay might have dried improperly. Barn fires were not that uncommon. Although Samuel had painted and changed the interior of the barn for her birthday last year, sometimes it still seemed as if Mr. Simms's shadow was still there. She was glad the barn was gone. Now there was nothing left to remind her of those days.

June 17, 1784

I feel like I am a decade older, not a year. The high-light of my week is coming to Emma's. Lucy plays more with the older boys than she does with Carrie. Carrie is content to try to herd the twins around. I do not know how Emma accomplishes all she does.

Lucy looked from the entry at the bottom of the page to the entry on the next. An entire year had passed. She held the book to catch the light. A page had been cut out. Why? She would have had her sixth birthday that year—the year she learned to dread the barn and the dark hours in the tack room. Had Mama written about the punishments but then removed them? Or was there something else she didn't want anyone to know? Lucy ran her finger down the gutter between the pages. She had been over the journal and the box enough times to know there were no loose pages. Perhaps her mother had burned the missing pages hoping to erase whatever they contained, and with the barn now gone, perhaps—a muffled cry came from the gathering room, and Lucy laid the book aside.

Samuel shut his ledger and pushed back from the table. The scrape of his chair startled Maryanna in her sleep. Lucy rubbed the baby's forehead to soothe her, wishing she could calm her husband as easily.

Samuel paced the room, rubbing his neck. "I could take out a loan. Pa suggested I build a smaller barn and a separate workshop, but it will cost more. At least Mr. Summers was understanding about his table being late."

"Can you work in your father's shop?"

"For a while, but it will be too crowded if we both have a large order. Do you know how blessed we are that almost everything was delivered by Christmas? Thank heaven for parties and family gatherings." Samuel stopped and stared into the fireplace. "But there still isn't enough money to rebuild."

"I have money." Lucy cooed at Maryanna as she moved her to the cradle. Samuel stood staring at her. Lucy grasped his hand and led him into the bedroom, stopping in front of the shelf holding her mother's box. "Mama saved this her whole life." She opened the box, pulled out the leather pouch, and set it in her husband's palm.

Samuel opened the bag and poured a few coins into his other palm. "This is a fortune. Where did she get it?"

Lucy led Samuel to the bed and sat down. "According to Mama's journal, it came from one of the men. He said he tried to stop the others and was the one who put a blanket on her. Mama felt that if she ever used it, it would be like they'd paid for that night." She bit her lip and waited for Samuel's reaction.

He poured the coins back into the pouch and handed it back to her. "I can't use it. The money is yours, or yours and Sarah's."

"Even if I split it with Sarah, there is more than enough to build a new barn and shop. There will even be some left over with that."

"I can't, Lucy. A husband should provide. It is yours."

Lucy's anger flashed as quickly as the flames that had consumed their barn. "What else would I spend the money on? Silks and china?"

Samuel didn't answer as he stood and left the room. Lucy heard the lean-to door shut and knew he was going to stare at the wreckage again. As she locked the money away, she wondered if she should hug him or slap some sense into him.

Nine

THE *CHEE-CHEE-CHEE* OF THE RATTLE and Maryanna's happy squeals
filled the house. Samuel left just after sunrise, Sarah in tow, to
help his father complete a table and chair set that was due the first
of February. Sarah was looking forward to being with Samuel's
brothers. Lucy hoped Thomas could talk some sense into Samuel
if the subject came up and if Samuel told him of her offer. There
was no reason to take out a loan when she had money she didn't
need just sitting there.

Why were men so stubborn? It felt good to give the bread dough
a few extra-hard punches before forming it into loaves. She hoped
it would still turn out after the abuse she'd given it.

With dinner preparations complete, Lucy sat down to read.

June 17, 1785

> *I do not write as often as I wish I could. I saw J's
> sister again. She didn't speak to me. I hear he is in
> Philadelphia. Welford dotes on his horses and hopes to
> turn Papa's farm into a breeding operation. He has let
> the south fields go unplanted this season for a pasture.
> He uses the others to grow hay. I cannot quite get used
> to the smaller garden now that there is no war.*

October 2, 1785

> *Lucy has started dame school. I am so happy to have*
> *her out of the house. Welford never calls her by name*
> *anymore. I let her play with Emma's children as often*
> *as I can, though she follows Samuel around more that*
> *she plays with Carrie. He is much like a big brother*
> *to her. She will be seven soon. I would not think at all*
> *on my seven years of marriage if I didn't think on her.*
> *There are other women much worse off than I am.*

Thunk. The rattle hit the floor. Maryanna blinked a few times at her empty hand before squeezing her eyes closed and opening her mouth. When Lucy picked her up and returned the rattle to her, Maryanna rewarded her with a toothless grin, though she promptly dropped the rattle again. Lucy bent to pick it up, and Maryanna laughed.

"Oh, you invented a new game." Lucy laughed at her daughter and indulged them both in a game of pick up the rattle until it was time for Maryanna to eat.

January 8, 1786

> *James was at church today. His father passed. He*
> *must be staying for a while. I think my heart has*
> *stopped. Welford acted the part of a doting husband—*
> *until we got home, where he hit me again and again*
> *before leaving on his horse. I pray he does not come*
> *back today. I have brought Lucy to Emma's. Though my*
> *excuse is weak, they will keep my girl for a few days.*

The taste of blood filled Lucy's mouth. Lucy checked to see if she'd bitten her lip, but it was only a memory. Mr. Simms had slapped her when she tried to stop him from hitting Anna, and her tooth had fallen out. It had been one of the tiny ones that would have come out anyway. Had she not been worried for Mama, the fact that she'd swallowed the tooth would have been more upsetting. The two had walked to the Wilson's in the lightly falling snow. Mama sang songs and tried to find happy things to look at. Lucy couldn't remember how long Mr. Simms was gone that time, but he bought Mama a new carriage. Even at the time it seemed silly. Mama never did drive one alone. Papa Marden sold the carriage for Mama soon after Mr. Simms's death.

April 6, 1786

Poor Lucy, the Garrett girl put ants in her lunch pail. Samuel found her crying at the side of the road as he came back from his school. He offered her one of his mother's maple-sugar candies for every ant she could catch next time. I don't want there to be a next time.

April 10, 1786

The teacher won't listen, and neither will Mrs. Garrett. She is the first woman to refer to Lucy being from the "wrong side of the blanket" since Lucy was born. She was at Mary's funeral and must know the truth. I must write to get it out. I do not want Welford to cause problems. And he surely will. He does allow Lucy the name Simms, after all.

June 17, 1786

I promised myself I would only write if good things happen.

September 10, 1786

We are leaving Lucy at Emma's for a week. Welford is taking me to Boston. He says a doctor there may have a cure for me. I pray it works this time.

November 3, 1786

Welford hasn't been drunk for three months. I fear it will end, though, when I tell him I was only later than usual. I am leaving Lucy here for the night. If only I could keep her as safe as my journal.

It hadn't occurred to Lucy how many times Mama had tried to protect her. Her mother's calm refusal to not fight back wasn't weakness.

No wonder she had spent almost as much time at the Wilson's as she had at home. Mama planned it that way.

Mothers did so much for their children, as she now knew from these past three months and to some extend the past year with Sarah. But most of those things were little—letting Sarah have the last piece of gingerbread or pacing back and forth all night with a sick baby. Every mother did these kinds of things. Why hadn't she known this while Mama still lived? All the anger she'd harbored over Mama's seeming indifference to Mr. Simms's harshness melted. What had occurred while Lucy was locked in that tack room? Was it that her mother didn't hear? Or was she locked in a place so much worse that Lucy was safer alone in the barn? The missing page probably hid the answer. Lucy was glad it was gone, afraid she didn't want to know the truth of it.

February 19, 1787

> *Welford has gone to Boston, or so he told everyone as he left town. Emma came to visit and found us. She has brought us to her home and sent Junior and Samuel to care for the farm. Lucy's back is a mess, as is mine, and I have bruises from his fists covering every inch of me. Today I can open my eyes but wish that I could not. My poor angel, and I can hardly hold her for the pain.*

> *I don't know what I would do without Emma. I feel much like I did that night nine years ago. Only then it took four to inflict this much pain. I watch Emma and Thomas and know in my heart that marriage can be happy. I wish that so much for my Lucy. But I fear for her future as she is learning never to smile.*

Sobs broke the silence. Lucy realized they were hers. The memories flooding back became nightmares. She needed Samuel. He would reassure her that all was well. He always did.

Lucy put the book away. If she were to read on, it would have to be with her husband beside her.

Samuel carried a sleeping Sarah into the house. Lucy did not look up as he passed her nursing in the rocking chair. Nor did she look up as he descended the stairs. "Sweetheart?"

Lucy raised her face, wet with tears, and blinked at him through red-rimmed eyes.

"Are you hurt? Is Maryanna?" Crossing the room in three strides, he knelt in front of the chair. Relieved to hear his daughter eating hardily, he turned all his attention to his wife. "Lucy?"

Her mouth opened, but no words came out. Samuel fumbled in his pocket for his handkerchief. Dirty from Sarah's muddy face. He grabbed a towel from near the dry sink and patted Lucy's face. *Was this over the money? Should he take it?*

"J-j-just memories."

"Oh, sweetheart," he said as he gently cupped her cheek in his hand. Maryanna stopped eating and looked at him. "Is she finished?" Before Lucy could finish nodding, he'd lifted the baby out of her arms, the swift movement startling a burp out of the baby. "Well, I guess you are done."

Holding her in one arm, he extended the other to his wife. Lucy stood and moved into his embrace. Samuel did his best to hold her and the baby at the same time. He should have left the last chair for tomorrow and come home an hour ago.

The nickering of a horse interrupted his thoughts. Lucy stepped back and looked toward the window. Movement in the shadows was the only other indication that the horses stood waiting to be unhitched.

"I need to…Can you?"

Lucy took Maryanna from his arms and nodded toward the door.

After delivering the horses to the nearest neighbors for the night, Samuel was back in the house, albeit winded, in less than half an hour. He found Lucy still rocking their sleeping child. Wordlessly he moved Maryanna to her cradle, then came back for Lucy, armed with a fresh handkerchief. He coaxed her into the parlor, where they could sit side by side.

Lucy took the proffered handkerchief. "She did so much to protect me, and I never knew. I remember her lying on top of me. Mr. Simms was so angry. Mama must have had scars too. I didn't know. Papa Marden truly understood when he said mine wouldn't matter to the right man. I didn't know. I blamed her for not doing enough." Lucy turned into his shoulder and cried.

Samuel held her, his hand purposely caressing her back, trying to reassure her once again that he loved her, scars and all. He hadn't thought about them or noticed them for months. Kissing the top of Lucy's head, he murmured, "James was right. They don't matter at all."

Lucy pulled back and dried her eyes. "I wish Mama would have talked about it before. Did you know he made her go to Boston to a doctor because she couldn't carry his child?"

A shudder moved up Samuel's spine. Not all doctors were as gentle as the one he'd apprenticed under. He tried not to imagine what type of treatment might have been inflicted on his mother-in-law. Bloodletting at the very least. A wave of nausea swept over him. Unable to answer, Samuel shook his head.

"I want to finish reading her journal, but it so hard. I know things will be better in a few more pages."

"Why don't you skip a few pages?"

"I don't want to miss where Papa Marden—"

"What if I read it and mark where you should start?'

Lucy stood up and left the room. A few minutes later she returned with the little book. "I ended at the ribbon. If you can just move it to the place where Mr. Simms…to where he . . ." She ended the sentence with a sigh.

Died. Samuel didn't need to say it out loud. The sigh said it all. Few had attended the funeral, and he could not recall anyone shedding tears for the man who had been thrown from a horse he'd surely been whipping. "The summer of '88?"

"Yes." Lucy left him alone to read.

Samuel read until he found the entry he was looking for.

July 20, 1788

> *I should be mourning. I dress as if I am. Welford is dead. Lucy and I are free. I am taking my box home.*

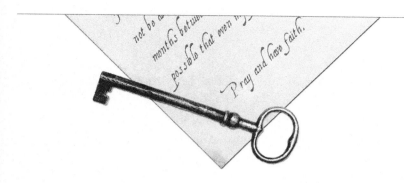

Ten

LUCY WATCHED SAMUEL AND HIS brothers clear the spot where the barn had stood. Most of the wood was ruined, but the small pile of useful boards was growing. Lucy turned to where Emma played with her granddaughter. "I wish Samuel would just take the money."

"What money?" Emma didn't look up from the hide-and-seek game she was playing with Maryanna.

"Mama's money. Even with half going to Sarah, it is enough to build a fine new barn and shop. Instead, he is going to build a small shed until he can expand." Lucy knew she was whining, but after two weeks of trying to get Samuel to use her money, she needed advice. "Mama kept it in the box you and Thomas gave her when she married Mr. Simms."

Emma shifted in her seat. "You found the key?"

Lucy nodded.

"May I ask if you know where the money came from?"

"The man who came to the church—the one you told me about. Mama wrote in her journal that he tried to stop them. He left the blanket and even offered to marry her. I don't think mother ever spent any of it." Lucy didn't want to discus that part of the story.

Maryanna yawned, momentarily capturing Emma's attention. "How long have you two been arguing about this money?"

"We haven't been arguing, exactly." Lucy transferred the cut-up potatoes to the pot.

Emma was silent for too long. Lucy looked up.

"Remind me. Why did Samuel call off the wedding?"

"Because of his fainting and leaving Harvard?"

"Partly."

Lucy looked Emma in the eye. "He thought he had no means to support a wife."

"Exactly. What does that tell you about Samuel?"

"He makes decisions without consulting me," Lucy said as she started to peel a carrot.

Emma swung the baby up to her hip. "Not that. The good part of his character."

Biting her lip, Lucy continued to work on the carrot. She set down the knife. "Samuel is very concerned about providing for the family."

Emma started to nod, but Maryanna grabbed her chin, and Emma nibbled at the little fingers, sending her granddaughter into a fit of giggles.

"Are you trying to tell me Samuel thinks that if he uses the money, it means I think he can't provide for us?"

Emma answered in a singsong voice as she continued to interact with Maryanna. "That could very well be. Your father doesn't view it as a gift, does he, little one?"

Maryanna babbled a reply.

"So how do I get him to see it as a gift?"

Emma stopped her game with the baby. "That is one question you must find the answer to yourself. Let me trade you. Your daughter needs some dry clothes."

Lucy smiled. Emma's duties as a grandmother only extended so far.

⇥ ❈ ⇤

Sarah set the broom aside. "I finished it again."

"That looks much better. Remember to always start with the corners when you clean. For some reason, it gets the whole floor cleaner."

Sarah tilted her head. "You sound just like Mama. She used to tell you that all the time."

Lucy laughed. "Yes, she did, didn't she? I always wanted to do something else. Knit, read, or sew a quilt. Anything but clean."

"Can I—I mean, *may* I go draw now?"

"Yes, but stay out of the mud."

"It's all mud." Sarah stood in the open doorway, clutching her drawing board.

"Then you will need to be very careful." Lucy said as she followed her onto the porch, but she doubted her sister heard the caution. The sun shone brightly. It was one of those February days masquerading as spring. Lucy wasn't fooled, though. There would be new snow by the end of the week. If it weren't so muddy, she would be tempted to carry Maryanna out for a walk, but her baby was sleeping. She could read out here. With the door open to air out the house, she would hear Maryanna. After all, it had been three weeks since she last opened the journal. Three weeks of contemplating the strength of character her mother had possessed and wishing once again that they could talk. And the sunshine put her in mind of Papa Marden's saying about problems looking better in the sunshine.

August 3, 1788

> *James was at church today. He nodded at me. When did he come back?*

August 4, 1788

James came by while I was milking. I didn't know what to say. He shooed me out of the barn and finished the chores.

August 10, 1788

James is living with his sister.

September 5, 1788

James came and mended a fence. Lucy shies away from him, but he is kind to her. I don't know what he wants, but I can't marry again. I am happier alone.

Laughter bubbled up inside Lucy. The frequent entries all began with James's name. Lucy remembered how flustered Mama would get. She started spending more time on her hair. It was not uncommon to come home from school and find Papa Marden doing some chore. Mama started baking pies and little cakes and on occasion invited him to supper. But then she would regret her impulsiveness and not allow him in the house for a couple of weeks. Looking back, Lucy realized that James treated Mama just like a good farmer treated a skittish horse—with constant little doses of affection until trust was earned.

December 12, 1788

James was surprised to learn that today is Lucy's tenth birthday. I don't think anyone has told him what everyone knows.

December 15, 1788

He knows. I am not sure if he pieced it together or if someone told him of Mary's death. The way he looked at me nearly undid me. He told me he understood my marrying Welford now. I think he wants to woo me into marrying him next. How can I tell him there is no future and that I am barren? I remember him talking about the large family he wished to have.

January 1, 1789

James touched my face, and I flinched. I tried to apologize. He was just moving a bit of my hair.

February 4, 1789

James kissed me. It was so much like the first kiss I remember. I am not sure why I am crying. Such an odd reaction.

March 3, 1789

He asked me to marry him. Lucy was at school. I told him I couldn't, and I told him more than I even told Emma about that night, about Welford and about being barren. I didn't mean to say so much, but he needed to understand about the men and Welford. When I was done, he just held me. Before he left, he said he would ask me again and again until I said yes.

I am afraid he will.

I am more afraid he won't.

April 10, 1789

He asked me again. I cried when I told him no. Then he kissed me on the forehead. I want to say yes. I am crying again.

May 3, 1789

James still comes every day and has done most of the planting. We sold off two of Welford's mares as I do not want to breed them. James has not asked me again, but he says there is no reason I should let the farm go while I make my decision. He has offered to buy the farm at a handsome sum if I choose not to marry him. That, with the money I have in the pouch, should see us through until Lucy is nearly twenty.

June 10, 1789

James hums "Lavender Blue" all the time. Does he know the naughty verses? I keep hearing "because I love you" in my mind when I see him.

June 17, 1789

He said yes. We were talking last night just as the stars came out. I didn't mean to ask him. It came out all wrong. I wondered if he was going to ask me again, and then he was saying yes and kissing me. We posted our intentions this morning. I think this the best birthday I have ever marked.

Lucy couldn't contain her laughter. Mama had proposed to Papa? Samuel stuck his head up from the boards he was cutting for the barn and then crossed the yard to the railing.

"Want to share?"

"Mama proposed to Papa Marden. Well, he proposed first, but she was the one to propose the last time." Lucy covered her mouth in an attempt to quiet her laughter.

Samuel crooked a finger and beckoned her over to the railing. "I say your mother was a smart woman. Too bad she didn't pass that on to her oldest daughter."

Lucy batted his shoulder.

Samuel easily caught her hand and kissed the back of it. "If her daughter would have proposed to me"—he turned her hand over and kissed her wrist—"I would have not had so much trouble"—he added a few more kisses—"last year."

Lucy ruffled his hair with her free hand. "If *Sarah* had proposed last year, you would have had much more trouble," she joked.

Samuel dropped her hand and took a step back. "You think so, my wench?" His voice took on the pirate growl she loved. With one bound he leaped over the railing and caught Lucy in his arms. The subsequent kiss he gave her was interrupted by Lucy's laughter.

She laid her hand on his chest. "Please, I am laughing too hard!"

Samuel moved his kisses to her jaw and neck. "Never tell a pirate to not kiss his bonny wench."

This time it was Maryanna's cries that interrupted them. Lucy gave him one more kiss before answering her daughter's call.

August 7, 1789

I am now Mrs. James Marden. He gave Lucy a new dress, and right after the reverend pronounced us man and wife, he scooped her up, hugged her, and gave her the choice of staying at the Wilson's or here. She is sleeping in the loft. James is in the barn. I am afraid.

September 10, 1789

I am not scared anymore. James is making plans to add on to the house. When I told him I wanted to keep my oven, he didn't argue the point at all. He repaired the roof leak and wondered why I had not told him of it all these months, but he wasn't angry. I feel as if I am in a bit of heaven.

October 11, 1789

I showed James my box. He agreed we should save the money for Lucy. He said he wished he had all the letters I had sent him so he could add them to the ones I kept, but he'd burned them when he found out I was married. I wish I could describe how I feel. It is as if I've been sick for a very long time and now I am well again. I fear my Lucy is not so fast to recover.

Papa Marden. Lucy missed him so much. He'd always tried so very hard to show her how much he loved her. Little everyday things like giving her the last bit of honey in the jar, declaring that he was not sweet enough to eat it. Or when he would buy her a dress length for her birthday and talk of the man her husband should be.

December 12, 1789

He took Lucy and me on a sleigh ride. Until Lucy laughed, I hadn't realized I hadn't heard that from her often. Then he gave Lucy her own little Bible.

March 3, 1790

I am with child. Emma confirmed it today. James is so happy. I think he is already building a cradle. For myself, I cannot believe it.

The cradle Papa Marden had made was currently in use in the bedroom. It was a fine piece of workmanship. Samuel had only to oil it to prepare it for Maryanna.

Lucy ran her hand over the smooth wood of her combination rocking chair/cradle, which sat in the gathering room. Samuel had sketched its design the very night she had told him of her suspicions. Good husbands did things like that, she mused. As if he had been reading her thoughts, Samuel entered the room carrying their daughter, who was trying to put her little hand in his mouth.

Lucy closed the journal. "What are you two doing?"

Samuel turned his head away from the exploring hand. "We were watching the falling snow, and Sarah was drawing on the windowpanes, until our little one decided to—I changed her cloths."

Maryanna slapped her father's chin. In turn, he nibbled on her little fingers, and squeals of delight filled the room.

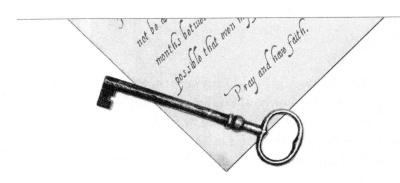

not be a ... months between ... possible that even in ... Pray and have faith.

Eleven

SAMUEL CHECKED THE SUMS IN his ledger once more. Without a shop of his own, it would be impossible to earn as much as he had last year. The cost of feed for the boarded animals was more than he expected. He replayed the conversation he'd had with his father earlier that day.

"Son, Old Brown is a fine horse. Why don't you pair him with one of the team?"

Samuel fed his horse a handful of oats. *"You know the answer to that. He wants to lead and is always trying to win some imaginary race with the other horse. It takes a lot of work to keep him in line. And when he is paired with a mare, he gets more interested in her than he should be."*

"Old Brown makes a great bachelor, but he wouldn't fare so well in marriage."

It had been a long time since his father had given him a lecture. Lucy must have said something to Ma about the money. He waited for his father to continue.

"Look at this team." Thomas waved to the set he used for most of the heavy hauling. *"If Kitty slows down, Pup will match her pace to haul the load evenly. If Pup strains at the load, Kitty will too. They work so well together that their names are even more ironic. Never*

let a three-year-old girl name your horses, son. But, remember, it is
a good thing to let your woman carry part of your load."

The lecture had ended as abruptly as it had started, giving Samuel even more to think about.

Samuel heard the lean-to door close. Lucy was back from the privy. He watched her cross the room with Sarah's drawing board in hand and a grin on her face.

"What did Sarah draw that has you smiling so?" Samuel reached for the board.

Lucy held the board out of his reach with one hand and hoisted the hem of her skirt with the other. "I gots me nuttin' for the likes of you. This here be a treasure map to a stash of pirate booty." She cackled in a voice more appealing than it was meant to be.

Samuel stood and closed one eye. "But I be the captain of this ship."

"And I be your bonnie wench, and I say you must take me with you if you take the map." Lucy planted both fists on her hips, keeping the drawing board slightly behind her.

Samuel looked at the stairs. They had sent Sarah to bed half an hour ago, and Lucy had laid Maryanna down only a few minutes after that. "Aye, me bonnie girl. Ye shall come with me. Think ye we need a lantern?"

Lucy shook her head. "No, Cap'n. It be a bright, waxing moon we'll see by." She set the board on the table and folded the paper.

Samuel bit back a chuckle as he put on his coat. Just what was his wife planning? Holding the door open, he followed Lucy out into the cold night air.

She squinted at the paper. "Cap'n, the map says to start at the biggest maple ye can see."

Samuel reached for Lucy's hand and led her to the biggest tree in the copse south of the house.

"Now ye must walk ten paces east."

Samuel took one giant step and stopped. "My paces be longer than yours. Does the map say which ones?"

His wife worried her lip. "Best use mine, sir." They counted out the paces together.

"Stand on the rock ye find there and look to the lavender vale."

Samuel stepped up on the small boulder and looked in the direction of the stream.

"Now, walk yerself back to the tune of 'Lavender Blue.'" They hummed the tune as they walked backward, ending near the corner of the burned-out barn.

"Now ye must dig."

"Why me?"

"'Cause you be the cap'n, sir."

"With what?'

Lucy pointed. "There be a shovel leaning on that pile of boards."

Samuel retrieved the tool and started digging where he could see the ground had been disturbed. On the third scoop, he hit something hard. Bending over the hole, he found a large rock. "What kinda treasure be this?"

"Mayhap ye should look under the rock," Lucy hinted, practically bouncing from foot to foot.

He lifted the rock and found a cracked crock underneath. As he lifted it out, he heard a soft clink. Reaching inside, he found a small cloth bundle. Anna's money. Samuel weighed it in his hand for a moment. It was not as heavy as the leather pouch. She must have divided it and left half for Sarah. He rolled to his feet and closed one eye before turning to his wife. "See here, my bonnie wench. We've struck treasure!"

Lucy clapped her hands, and Samuel grabbed her about the waist. "I think ye have been trying to fool the captain. How shall I punish ye?"

Lucy's eyes widened, and she tried to step back.

"I think I shall steal a kiss for every coin ye hid."

Samuel realized later that he should have counted the coins first, but Lucy didn't seem to mind her double punishment.

April 6, 1790

    James has started on the addition. He wants it fin-
ished before the baby is born. Lucy smiles more often
now. She no longer follows Samuel around. I think they
are both growing up. Maybe someday he will treat her
like James treats me.

"Oh, Mama, he does, he does," Lucy whispered, hoping that
somehow her mother would know. "He is building a new barn and
shop with that money. It will be good not to see Mr. Simms's barn
anymore." Lucy returned to her reading.

July 12, 1790

    Is it wrong that a wife think her husband per-
fect? I know he has some faults, but after Welford,
he is perfect. He gave me the loveliest cameo to mark
my birthday.

September 8, 1790

    Benjamin is here. We named him after James's father.
He cries ever so much. I knew Lucy was an angel of a
baby. He has his father's nose. I never thought I could
be this happy.

A smile came to Lucy's face. She had been so excited to have
a brother. It had given her a chance to use her cooking skills, too.
And not once had Papa Marden scolded her over the burned bread
or not-so-cooked beans. Mama had instructed her on changing
the baby's cloths. Papa Marden was the first to make a mistake

and have Benjamin water his face. At the thought, Lucy stifled a laugh lest she wake Maryanna. Girls were easier in that regard. Mama was the only one Benjamin had not drenched at one time or another. After a month, Mama insisted Lucy return to school, but no one had cared much to listen to her prattle on about her baby brother.

The lean-to door creaked. Samuel must be coming in. He had taken to using that door so he could remove his heavy boots and not wake Maryanna when she slept. Lucy set the journal down on the seat of the rocker and went to greet him.

Samuel slipped into her arms. "Is that smile for me or for something else?"

Lucy planted a quick kiss on his cheek. "Always for you, but I was reading Mama's journal and remembering Benjamin as a baby. Someday I hope—" It was too forward to speak of having another child so soon. Lucy gave a tiny shrug instead of finishing the thought.

Samuel slipped his arm around Lucy's waist and spun them both into the great room. He bent his head low. "I see our little lady is sleeping. Now what do you hope?" The rakish tilt of his head caused Lucy to think only of kissing him, so she did.

"Hmmm. I hope we have a son too."

Lucy studied Samuel's face. How had he known?

"How long do you think our little one will sleep?" Samuel nodded in the direction of the rocker cradle.

Lucy looked at the clock. "A least an hour."

"And Sarah will not be home for two from my mother's." Samuel's eyes darkened, and his kisses deepened. With each one, he spun them closer to the bedroom door.

Lucy didn't mind not being able to read more today.

⚒ ❈ ⚒

There were only a few entries left. Lucy skimmed over the few that dealt with the farm and days she remembered. She found herself stopping only to read when her name was mentioned.

April 12, 1792

> *I am with child again. I am glad Lucy is here to help. It seems that every smell makes me ill.*

April 17, 1792

> *Benjamin nearly walked into the fire today, but Lucy grabbed him in time. James is carving him a horse. I hope it keeps him occupied.*

September 1, 1792

> *Lucy taught Benjamin to feed the chickens. I think he can run as fast as she does. How will I keep up with this one?*

October 24, 1792

> *Sarah looks much like Lucy did. But she screams worse than Benjamin and at only two weeks old. Emma says it is colic and has advised that I give her a bit of peppermint tea from a spoon. Mrs. H says I should put warm cloths on her stomach. And Mrs. G questions if it is my milk and suggests I get a nurse or a goat.*

December 12, 1792

*Lucy looks so grown-up in her new dress. I can
hardly believe she is fourteen. I think Samuel notices
her in a different way as their bantering has ended. Oh,
I pray that in four or five years such good friends will
find felicity in marriage.*

Lucy couldn't help but smile. Did Mama ever look down from
heaven and see that her prayers had been answered? Not that everything was perfect. Samuel often let his whiskers grow out too long
and often forgot to come in for dinner if he was in the middle of
a project. Before next winter, Lucy planned to buy a bell so she
wouldn't have to traipse out to the new shop he was building closer
to the road.

Samuel was such a diligent worker. Winter or not, he had managed to raise a new barn with the help of several others. It was much
smaller than Mr. Simms's monstrosity but more than adequate for
their needs.

June 17, 1793

*Sarah slept through the night. I couldn't have asked
for a better way to mark my birthday. Although James
did spoil me with a new gown and slippers.*

September 20, 1793

*Another child so soon? Sarah is not yet weaned. But
Emma agrees with me—I shall present James with
another child in the spring. And to think I was so sure
I was barren. Perhaps it was because Welford did not
show me the kindness James does. Although that would
not explain Lucy. I dreamed of them again. It has been*

such a long time since I dreamed like that. Perhaps it was because James went to Gloucester for two days for his mother's funeral. Lucy still has an occasional bad dream about Welford. I wish…it doesn't matter what I wish. It won't change what was. I am just so happy for my "what is."

Lucy paused to ponder that. *Happy for my "what is."* There were so many bad parts to life—not just things like Mama's terrible things, but day-to-day bad. Illness, the barn fire, and even death. If she had known Papa Marden's kindness only, would she cherish Samuel's as much? Or was it her memories of Mr. Simms that made her appreciation grow? Mama's writings indicated she cherished James more after her life with Mr. Simms than as an infatuated sixteen-year-old. Perhaps that was one of the secrets of Mama and Papa Marden's happiness—it had come from difficult things.

March 18, 1794

Wondering if I should tell Lucy about Mary and that night. Emma says I should. I rather let things alone as I don't like talking about it. Emma says Lucy needs to understand why Welford called her those names. But I don't want to give her more nightmares.

June 6, 1794

This baby is almost too quiet. She is so much like Lucy was. I watch Lucy hold her and think that I was just about her age when Lucy was born. She will be a good mother. Emma says—

Whatever Anna meant to write, the entry ended there. Had Emma been worried about little Jane's health, then? Or had Mama just been interrupted?

October 22, 1794

> *Lucy is moping about. Samuel has left for Cambridge to become a doctor. I don't know that I could get through the day without her help. She is young to marry yet.*

December 15, 1794

> *James told me someone asked to court Lucy. James denied him. I know not who it was, but I suspect Mr. Sidewell as he has been desperate for a new wife since Hester's passing. Lucy has just turned sixteen this week. She is far too young to mother those boys. Samuel is getting on well at Harvard. He is here for the month. Emma and I still have hopes for him and Lucy, although they seem to barely talk.*

Mr. Sidewell had asked to court her? Papa Marden had never said a word about it. If she could hug Papa Marden right now, she would. What an odious man, that Abner Sidewell. The entire town had breathed a collective sigh when he'd left with his boys for Ohio or some such place during the summer. She was glad her friend Elizabeth had been spared being wed to him too. That reminded her—she did owe Elizabeth a letter. She glanced at the clock. There was maybe half an hour before Maryanna would demand to be nursed. She should get out the writing desk and write to her friend.

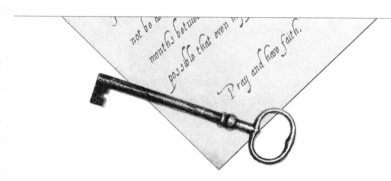

Twelve

"THAT IS A SPARROW." LUCY pointed Maryanna's pudgy hand toward the treetop. "And do you hear that? That is a mockingbird."

Maryanna lay her head on Lucy's shoulder and stuck her thumb in her mouth.

"Are you tired?"

Of course there was no reply, but the babe's heavy eyelids were answer enough. Lucy crossed the yard and settled her daughter in the basket on the porch.

Having completed her tasks for the day, she resolved to finish reading the journal.

July 20, 1795

> *I had a moment to ponder my family today as James read from the Bible and I sat nursing Jane. I find I am content as all the things I ever wished for as a young girl are currently here, in this very room. Lucy is holding Sarah, and Benjamin is laughing at his father's tales of his youth. Ten years ago, I could not believe that someday I would have laughter in my home. Maybe it is the anniversary of Welford's passing that makes me*

reminisce so. I fear there are none who visit his grave. I am glad I did not bury him on the hill.

September 13, 1796

Little Jane is so very sick. I wonder if she shall be my first to die.

March 25, 1797

We buried Jane today. Poor Sarah looks for her sister and playmate in every room. She doesn't seem to understand that death is forever.

June 20, 1797

Emma's Carrie was wed this morning. I think Samuel will not be far behind if he can get Lucy to consent. I know she likes him, but something holds her back. I fear Welford's shadow comes to her from beyond the grave. James has tried to help Lucy. I hope his example is enough.

I have been so busy helping Emma I didn't write on my birthday. I am increasing again. I am just as ill as I was with Benjamin. I hope it is another son.

Mama had been right. Mr. Simms had been such a big part of the reason Lucy could not accept Samuel as a husband. If not for Papa Marden's encouragement, she would have never accepted Samuel's proposal. But as it had been made by letter and from so far away, it was easier to accept. Lucy doubted that if the original proposal had come in a more traditional way she could have said yes. It was so much easier to answer on paper.

August 27, 1797

Lucy and Samuel have posted their intentions, though they say they will not marry until next spring. I think they may wed when he takes a break in December.

September 17, 1797

James's sister has asked for Lucy to help this next month for her lying-in. The house seems empty without her, but with two other children, it is hardly quiet.

September 23, 1797

Samuel is back, and something is wrong. I don't know if Lucy knows what it is.

November 20, 1797

Benjamin died today of fevers and chills, but Sarah recovered from the same last week. The snow is falling, but surely it is too early for a blizzard.

Lucy swallowed a sob. Those days had been so difficult. Every new hour brought more heartache. Although both Emma and Samuel had assured her that the outcome would have been the same had she been able to get help, it did not ease her sorrow. The illness and harsh winter seemed to have had a relentless appetite for the lives of her loved ones. First little Jane, and then Benjamin, and then—

November 25, 1797

> My James is now dead. I fear the baby I carry will come early. But more than that, I fear leaving my girls alone. They cannot keep up the farm alone. I know that desperation! I hope Lucy makes a better choice than I did. My decision to marry Mr. Simms led to ten years of pain. If only Samuel weren't acting like a petulant child, as Emma puts it. Lucy harbors her pain too deeply, and he will have to try very hard to repair the damage of the broken engagement, if it is broken. As long as it isn't Abner Sidewell, I shall be content. I must tell her today of things I had hoped to forget.

Lucy closed the journal and used her apron to dry her tears. They had never had a conversation that day. Mama had tried to say a few things but lacked the strength.

"Sarah?" Lucy returned the journal to the box. When the time was right, she would share it with her sister. "Sarah?"

"I'm here." Only a couple of feet away, Sarah stood with her you-didn't-need-to-shout face on.

"I didn't hear you. Will you listen for Maryanna? I need to take a walk."

"Have you been crying?"

Lucy nodded. "Don't worry, dear. I am well enough."

A breeze swayed the green-tinged branches on the trees that stood over the graves on the hill. She paused at the graves of Aunt Mary and her sister Jane before she reached the five-foot-high, four-sided stone marker Samuel had commissioned the for grave that past summer.

Lucy traced the letters as she read them silently.

JAMES MARDEN
1759–NOVEMBER 25, 1797
PROBLEMS LOOK SMALLER IN THE SUNSHINE
✝

ANNA STICKNEY MARDEN, HIS BELOVED WIFE
1761–NOVEMBER 27, 1797
✝

BENJAMIN, THEIR FIRST SON
1790–NOVEMBER 20, 1797
✝

JAMES JUNIOR, WHO LIVED BUT A MOMENT
NOVEMBER 27, 1797
✝

THEY GO BEFORE US AND WATCH OVER US DAILY.

A pair of praying hands was carved near the base of the stone. Lucy traced them, too.

"Oh, Mama, I miss you so! I found the key. Thank you for writing. I wish we could have talked before you died. And, Papa Marden—" Words wouldn't come, but tears did. Tears for the hugs she could have given and the burdens she could have shared. Tears of gratitude for her mother and for all the things she would have done to help Anna had she known. Tears that she couldn't change what had been. And tears knowing that if the past were different, so, also, would the present—Samuel, Maryanna, Sarah, even the barn.

Strong arms encircled her from behind, and, sinking into his embrace, Lucy let Samuel pull her tightly against his chest. After several minutes, she turned toward him, most of her tears spent. He smelled of freshly sawed wood. More tears fell for a painful kind of joy at the things that placed her in his embrace.

Samuel kissed the top of her head. "You finished the journal."

Lucy nodded. As Samuel tightened his embrace, the sounds of early spring filled Lucy's ears against the backdrop of her husband's heartbeat. The little creek beyond the hill gurgled, and birds called to each other as they built their nests in the trees above.

Lucy stepped back just far enough to place a kiss on her husband's lips. "Thank you. I think I may start a journal of my own. But I shall start with the day my mother stopped by making a long entry about all that has happened in the past year. Mama wrote about the importance of not worrying over the past and being happy for what we have. I've spent so much time focusing on the bad that I didn't realize how much good had come in spite of it—and maybe because of it. Remember what you said about if things were different you wouldn't have me?"

She felt Samuel nodding against the top of her head.

"What if illness had not come to us last year? Would you have ever married me? Without the barn fire, would you be building such a modern, new shop? Would my precious Maryanna be less dear to me had she not been ill? I cannot answer these things, but I do know Mama believed that though there would be much of bad, God could change bad into good. There were times she promised to only write about the good, but then she wrote about the bad also. I think if I write my own journal, I will remember to be happy."

Lucy nestled into the warmth of his arms.

"And what will you write of me?" His voice was becoming husky.

Lucy turned to look over their house and farm, and a smile formed on her lips. "I shall write that my husband is sometimes stubborn and has to be tricked into making the right choices."

Samuel stiffened. "Tricked?"

"Didn't your parents trick you when we were first wed? And did it not take trickery to get you to accept the funds to make that fine new shop?" Lucy started to point, when Samuel gently placed his fingers on her chin and turned her back toward him.

His face transformed into a one-eyed glower. "Then this pirate will have to steal the fair lady's journal and amend it."

Lucy laughed as she always did when Samuel played the swash-buckler. And like a true pirate, he stole a kiss that guaranteed he would be given more.

The End

Historical Notes

RELATIVELY FEW JOURNALS, LETTERS, OR other writings exist today of women who lived during the American Revolution. Readers who are familiar with even a few of these documents will point out that, I erred by having Anna's journal written in standardized English with American spellings. I assure you this was a choice, after reading Laurel Thatcher Ulrich's *A Midwife's Tale* (which I highly recommend,) and other period documents I chose clarity and ease of reading over historical accuracy assuming that most readers would be reading this work for enjoyment rather than learning.

Writing crossed letters or crosshatching, became popular during the early nineteenth century as a way to save money on paper and postage by rotating the original letter ninety degrees and writing over it. Not only was this frugal but it was also used as a mark of friendship or even romance. I included this in Anna and James's war time correspondence in crossed writing as it is entirely plausible that such letters were drafted out of necessity before they became a part of Regency English life and subsequently a fashionable way to respond to a lover.

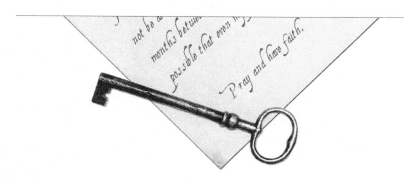

Acknowledgments

THERE ARE NOT ENOUGH WAYS to thank those who helped me bring about this book. Although I did not force my mother to read and reread this book she remains one of my best cheerleaders.

Huge thanks to my beta readers; especially Emily for her willingness to fit me in to her busy schedule. Sally, and Cindy, whose ideas, critiques and daily advice keep me going. Thanks to all the writers in Cache Valley League of Utah writers, and iWriteNetwork, each of you has made me a better writer. Thank you for your part in my growth as a fledgling writer.

Thanks also to Michele at Eschler Editing for the edits and finding oh so many little things to fix; any mistakes left in this book are not her fault. Nor are my excellent proof readers to be blamed. Thank you ladies!

My family, for sharing their home with the fictional characters who often got fed better than they did. And my husband who encouraged me every crazy step of the way, and who is my example for every love story I dream up. The real one is better.

And to my Father in Heaven for putting these wonderful people, and any I may have forgotten to mention, in my life. I am grateful for every experience and blessing I have been granted to form my life.

About the Author

LORIN GRACE WAS BORN IN Colorado and has been moving around the country ever since, living in eight states and several imaginary worlds. She graduated from Brigham Young University with a degree in Graphic Design.

Currently she lives in northern Utah with her husband, four children, and a dog who is insanely jealous of her laptop. When not writing Lorin enjoys creating graphics, visiting historical sites, museums, and reading.

Lorin is an active member of the League of Utah Writers and was awarded Honorable Mention in their 2016 creative writing contest short romance story category. Her debut novel, *Waking Lucy,* was awarded a 2017 Recommend Read award in the LUW Published book contest.

You can learn more about her and sign up for her newsletter at loringrace.com

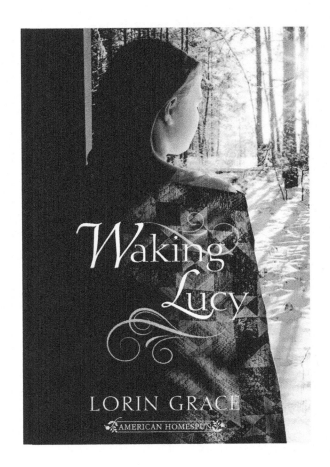

Waking Lucy

Lucy dreamed of marrying Samuel,
until she woke up as his wife.

Don't miss the first book in the series.

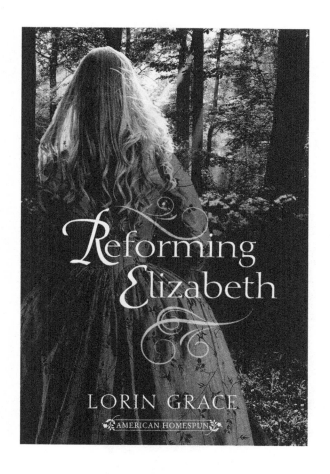

Reforming Elizabeth

Elizabeth Garret is out of control.
Can her great aunt and a disgraced preacher
succeed in reforming her?

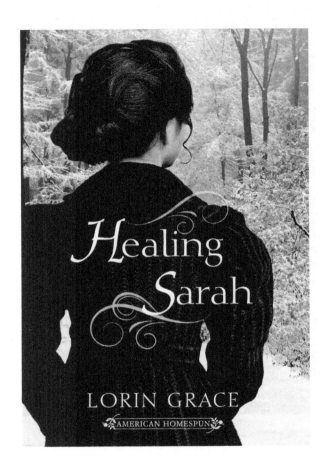

Healing Sarah

Summer 1816 never came.
The only thing colder is Sarah's heart.
Timison can heal Sarah if given the chance.

FRIDAY NIGHT ART SOCIETY

MENDING
FENCES

LORIN GRACE

Mending Fences

The fence that once brought
them together
now keeps them apart.

Contemporary Romance

Made in the USA
Monee, IL
01 July 2023